He Found Me

Joy Mullett

J M Publications Limited

To my family and friends who have always believed in me.
To you, the reader, thank you for giving my work a chance.
To the universe, for making my dreams come true.

Contents

Books in this series:

I've Found Her - Bella and Damien
I've Found Her part 2 - Chloe and Josh
He Found Me - Katie and Leo
She Found Me - Marco and Mia

With more to come from Katie and Leo later in the year.

All books are available on Amazon.

Follow Joy on social media @jemullettbooks for her latest releases and updates.

Authors Note

Please be aware this book is intended for mature audiences ages 18 and over.

The story includes open door romance, along with some darker themes, including kidnapping, violence and murder.

However, the main focus is on romance and a protective alpha male.

If you are okay with this, please continue and enjoy!

Joy x

He Found Me

By Joy Mullett

Chapter 1

Katie

Don't you just love waking up in the morning? Feeling all warm, cosy, and relaxed. Stretching out my arms, I feel the broad shoulders of my boyfriend, Jax. Slowly opening my eyes, I'm greeted by the morning sun peeking in around the blinds. I'm at Jax's place; it's where I spend most of my nights now. Jax begins to wake up too; he turns and pulls me into him.

"Good morning, beautiful."

Smiling, I snuggle into his arms. I love waking up like this. Jax smells amazing. I've no idea what aftershave he uses, but he still smells of it in the morning, along with his sexy manly scent. Running my hand over his head and down the back of his neck, I enjoy the feeling of his short hair against my palm. His dark green eyes are now wide open, watching me with that intense stare the way he does just before he is about to devour me. With tattoos from his neck down to his wrists, he can be quite scary looking if you don't know him. But I know him—every delicious bit of him.

Climbing on top of him for a better view, I trace the tattoos across his chest. His nipples harden while a groan escapes his throat. I bend to kiss his eager, strong lips, but just as I reach them...

BOOM! A loud bang echoes through the building.

Jax instantly throws me off him. I fly across the room with such force, my body collides with the radiator. My head hits the hard metal corner, and I feel my skin split on impact.

"Ouch!" Looking up, I see Jax in his boxers, pointing a gun at the closed bedroom door. A gun? Where the hell did he get a gun from? Jax doesn't own a gun. Does he?

"Police, stand back!" a stern voice orders through the door.

The bedroom door breaks off its hinges and falls to the floor at Jax's feet.

"Drop your weapon!" Three large police officers wearing full riot gear aim their huge terrifying-looking guns at Jax. Jax drops his gun and puts his hands in the air. Two more officers in normal uniforms enter the bedroom. They read him his rights, put him in handcuffs, and escort him out of the room. I can't believe the scene in front of me. Just five minutes ago, I was happy, content, and safe—or so I thought.

"Jax, what's going on?" I demand.

But Jax doesn't say a word. He exits the bedroom without even a glance towards me.

"Katie?"

My name makes me jump. I hadn't noticed the police lady standing beside me.

"You need to come with me. You have one minute to get dressed; then we will go to the station." She hands me my dressing gown and points to the bathroom.

After grabbing some clothes off the chair, I enter the bathroom and lock the door behind me. Staring at my reflection, I shake my head in disbelief. This must be some kind of mistaken identity. When the police read Jax his rights, they said something about theft and murder. There's no way Jax would have done anything like that. Splashing my face with some water, I put on a brave face. I quickly brush my teeth and I'm good to go.

The policewoman bangs on the door. "Katie, we need to leave!"

I put my gym pants on and pull my hoodie over my head. "Ouch." I had forgotten about the bang on my head. The bathroom lock turns, and the door opens. She's obviously had enough of waiting for me and unlocked the door from her side.

"What's taking so long?" Noticing the blood on my hands, as I have just touched my head, she comes in to inspect it. "It's not too bad. Come on; we've got a nurse at the station who will sort that out."

Down at the police station, after the nurse has cleaned and glued my head, I'm taken to an interview room.

"Can you state your full name, please?" the interviewer asks.

"Katie Harris," I reply nervously.

"Can you tell me how you know Mr. Jaxon Adams?"

"He's my boyfriend."

"How long have you been in a relationship with Mr. Adams?"

"About six months." I try to remain calm.

"Are you aware of what Mr. Adams does for a living?" He leans back in his chair, tapping his pen against his lips.

"Yes, he is a lorry driver."

"And what makes you think that is his occupation?" There's a sarcastic tone to his voice.

"He told me."

"Do you know the name of the company he

works for?"

"Umm, no, I don't."

"No? Why not?"

"I never asked."

"You never asked." The interviewer has a smirk on his face as he writes my answers on his notepad. "Have you ever been to his workplace or seen him driving a truck?"

"No, I haven't. But it's not like he would drive his truck home and park it on the drive, is it?" I am getting annoyed by his attitude.

"The house you were in this morning—who does that belong to?"

"Jax."

"Are you aware how much the houses in that area of London are worth, Miss Harris?"

What type of questions are these? I don't see how this is relevant.

"I'm not sure."

"In excess of two million pounds."

"Wow."

"Wow, indeed. And you think a lorry driver owns a house of that value?"

"I'm sorry, I am not sure what you are implying here?"

The interviewer leans forward in his chair,

placing his arms on the table and twiddling his pen in his fingers. This is so surreal. My heart is racing. I feel like I need to be careful about what I say. I feel guilty, even though I have done nothing wrong.

"Where were you on Saturday the 23rd of December, between the hours of 12:00 and 3:00 p.m.?"

"I was working at Bella Hairdressing. In The King Hotel."

"The King Hotel? You answered that quickly and specifically, considering it was over four months ago, Miss Harris."

"Yes, well, I'm a hairdresser, and the Saturday before Christmas is the year's busiest day in my industry. That week before Christmas, I spend my days in the salon and any rest time in my accommodation, which is also in the King Hotel. I am sure the whole building has CCTV, so you will be able to confirm that."

After what seemed like hours of more questions, they finally let me go. I haven't seen Jax, and nobody will tell me what is going on.

When I get back to Jax's house I break down. I can't believe the mess the police have left it in. They have taken everything out of every drawer and every cupboard. The house is ultra-modern and minimalistic, but it still looks like a bomb has gone off. Collapsing on the sofa, I let myself cry until all my tears have dried up. Frustration fills me. I need to speak to Jax. This is a massive misunderstanding. Jax cannot be responsible for what the police are saying. He can't be.

After I am all cried out, I put the house back together. Well, as best I can, we've only been together for six months. He gave me a key about a month ago; having spent most nights here, I have a bit of an idea of where things go. As I wander about the house, putting things back where I think they belong, I look at all his possessions. It never crossed my mind before, but everything in this house is worth a fortune, from the smart appliances in the kitchen to the paintings on the wall. I've just googled one artist, and his work sells for hundreds of thousands apiece. Then there's Jax's office, which had three computers in it. Well, at least I think it was three. I've only ever been in there once; he keeps it locked "just in case," he says. Just in case of what? I do not know. What does a lorry driver need an office for, anyway? How has he afforded all this? He hasn't really spoken much of his family. Maybe they are wealthy and buy him things? Goodness knows. I just wish I could speak to him. I miss him; I'm so worried about him.

It's well into the early hours when I'm finished tidying up, so I get in Jax's bed. The tears flow as I breathe in his scent off his pillow.

My alarm goes off at 7:00 a.m. I smile as my

eyes open, thinking it's all a dream—until I reach over to Jax's side of the bed to find it empty and cold.

I use the shower, get dressed, lock up, and go to my apartment to change and get ready for work. I still haven't heard from Jax. I ring the police station, but they don't tell me anything I don't already know.

At work, my brave poker face seems to have everyone fooled other than my manager, Bella, but she is one of my best friends.

As soon as she asks me what's wrong, I burst into tears. I don't tell her the whole truth, as I'm not sure what is true and what isn't right now; not being able to face any lectures, I say, "Jax left me yesterday morning and hasn't spoken to me since." It's not a lie. I'm just leaving out a lot of detail.

"Oh no, Katie. Come here." Bella gives me a hug, and I cry it out. She asks if I want to take some time off, but I don't. Being here helps to take my mind off things.

The next couple of days are a blur. I am sick with worry, but I put on a happy face while my mind works in overdrive.

When I finish work on Friday, I realise I haven't collected my post from my mailbox in a while. All the apartments have their own mailboxes at the hotel reception. When I get down there, I find it much fuller than usual, even for a few days' worth of post.

As I look through the pile, I realise they are birthday cards. Oh my goodness, tomorrow is my birthday. My thirtieth birthday. With everything that has been going on, it completely slipped my mind. Not feeling like opening them now, I leave them in my apartment and go to Jax's house. I let myself in, looking for any signs of life or that Jax may have been home. But no. I'm not sure why I'm disappointed. I didn't expect to find him here. I'm sure he will ring me the moment he gets released.

I put on Jax's favourite hoodie, grab my comfort teddy, Snuggly, out of my bag and get into his bed.

I must have fallen asleep for a few hours, because I wake to the sound of my phone ringing, its screen illuminating the dark room.

"Hello?"

"Katie, It's me."

It's Jax, thank goodness.

"Jax, where are you? Are you okay?"

"I'm fine. Where are you, Katie?"

I'm so relieved to finally speak to him, but I'm confused by the harsh tone of his voice. "I'm at your place; I'm actually in your bed; I miss y—"

Jax cuts me off. "You need to leave now," he

instructs firmly.

"What, why? Jax, I don't understand?" As I speak, I hear a knock on the door.

"I don't have time to explain. Just get your stuff and get out."

"Just a second. I think there's someone at the door." I look out of the window and see a Range Rover parked outside. There's a man in dark clothing standing at the front door. Another man looks to be walking around the back of the house.

"Listen to me carefully." Jax speaks firmly and quickly. "Some bad people have framed me. I don't have time to go into detail, but you need to leave and take all of your things with you. Do you understand? Everything. They cannot know I have a girlfriend, or they will come after you."

"O-okay," I stutter, my breathing becoming erratic.

"Seriously, Katie. Take everything. Your toothbrush and the tatty teddy you take with you everywhere. It all must be gone."

I have never heard Jax talk so abruptly, and it scares me.

I do as he asks, gathering all my things and throwing them into my bag. There's not much of mine here, just a few toiletries and some clothes, which are all neatly together in his drawer, thanks to me tidying up after the police made a mess.

"One of them has gone around the back. How do I get out?" I whisper into the phone I'm still holding against my ear.

"Go up into the loft. There's a hole in the left-hand side that leads to Mrs. Johnson's. Leave via her house, and don't go back there again."

"Okay, but—"

Jax cuts me off again. "I mean it, Katie. Do not go there again!"

My phone beeps, and the call ends. I stare at my phone in disbelief. Another loud knock on the door brings me back to reality. With a quick check around to ensure I have everything, I fumble through the dark, trying to find the loft hatch. The ladder to the hatch slides down with a screech. I hate lofts, especially in the dark. They have a funny musty smell and an eery feel about them. The ladder is very heavy to lift, but I manage to get it back up with a struggle. The latch closes just as I hear the back door being bashed off its hinges.

I sit still for a few moments, listening. My heart races and thuds in my ears. The two men are both in the house. I can hear them speaking to each other, but they're too far away for me to make out what they are saying. The sound of furniture being moved around makes me move. They're obviously looking for something.

I need to get out of here. Now that my eyes have gotten used to the dark, I make my way through the storage boxes as quietly as I can. I see the opening next door and climb through it. Mrs. Johnson's loft has a lot more stuff in it than Jax's. I can hardly move through the old furniture and creepy paintings. I locate the hatch to the house; it opens with a creak. I climb down the ladder while trying to think of an explanation as to why I have sneaked into Mrs. Johnson's house through her loft. Maybe she won't notice, and I can just quietly leave through the front door.

No such luck. As I close the hatch, she appears behind me.

"Hello, dear."

I turn with a jump.

"Mrs. Johnson, hi. I'm so sorry to intrude on you like this."

"Is Jax not with you?" Mrs. Johnson strains to look behind me, looking disappointed when she realises it's just me.

"No…. He's… away at the moment."

"Ahh, that's a shame; I haven't seen him for a while. I miss our chats." Mrs. Johnson is an eighty-year-old widow who has a soft spot for Jax. Every time I come over, there is a homemade dish in the fridge, courtesy of the friendly neighbour.

"Will you be staying for a cup of tea, or do you need to rush off?"

Something tells me this isn't the first time

someone has come through her loft unannounced.

"I need to get going. But thank you so much for the offer; I really am sorry to bother you."

"Anytime, dear. You tell Jax I have a currant bun with his name on it."

I quickly check the coast is clear and make my exit. Walking as fast as I can without drawing attention to myself, I don't stop until I am home.

It's Saturday. My birthday. I really don't feel like getting out of bed, let alone celebrating. If it wasn't for my clients booked in at the salon, I would stay in bed. I don't like letting people down. I drag myself out of the covers, and I get into the shower. I haven't slept a wink, but after a shower and a full face of makeup, you'd never know. With five minutes to spare before I need to leave, I open my birthday cards. There's one from my mum with a voucher for my favourite makeup and one from my dad, containing money.

The next one I open isn't a birthday card; it is a wedding invitation, along with a plane ticket. I read the bride and groom's names a few times, not recognising who they are. Confused, I check to see who it is addressed to on the envelope; it's definitely for me—my address, my name. It takes a few more minutes for it to register. But it can't be, can it? The bride... is me.

This is an invitation to my own wedding.

Chapter 2

Katie

I'm in a complete daze. My team at work has arranged a full day of surprises at the salon. I've been spoiled with gifts and food. There's been activities and games happening throughout the day. Everyone's dancing and singing while going about their day, but I cannot focus on anything. I am working on autopilot, carrying out colours and cuts on my clients; my head is somewhere different. Everyone keeps saying I'm overwhelmed with what's going on.

I am overwhelmed, all right, but not with my birthday celebrations. I am trying to get my head around why someone would send me a wedding invitation and a one-way ticket to Naples, Italy. The invitation is to the wedding of Katherine Harris and Leonardo Guerra. My full name is Katherine Harris. My dad has always called me Katie, so since I moved in with him at sixteen, I haven't been known as anything else. Only family and people who knew me before then would know that.

But it's the name Leonardo Guerra that my mind keeps being drawing back to. It's a surname I have been trying to remember for years. Guerra—how could I forget?

My first love, at fifteen years old—his name was Leonardo Guerra. My Leo.

Fifteen years ago.

"Kat-er-een!" Leo shouts through the fence that borders the hotel Mum and I are staying in.

My stomach fills will butterflies as I walk over to him. He's so incredibly handsome. I've never felt this way about a boy before.

"No person can see me, yes?" Leo's broken English makes me smile.

"The coast is clear." I beckon him to climb over.

"The coast?" He looks at me in confusion.

"I mean yes—there is nobody here, only me. No one can see you."

He smiles and jumps the fence. As soon as he reaches me, he cups my face in both hands. His dark eyes connect with mine before he kisses me so passionately. His kiss is firm, but his lips are gentle. We stay like that for a few seconds. The feeling of his lips on mine and his hands on my face make me feel lighter than air.

When he breaks our contact, my body protests, but then he puts his arm around me and calls me "La mia ragazza." My girl—and I melt into his arms. Which is where I spend most of the day. It's where I've spent every day since I met him—in his arms.

We walk over to our usual place in the hotel's gardens. There's lots of trees and tall plants, which give us the privacy Leo wants. Here we are in our own little world. Lying on the grass, I talk of my dream of being a hairdresser in a top hairdressing salon. Leo listens intently to my every word. He speaks much better English than I do Italian, but he is still learning. My fourteen days holiday in Italy are passing so quickly.

"Are you hungry?" I ask Leo. It's become our routine now that I go into the dining room of the hotel, fill a plate with food, and we share it beneath the palm trees.

"Yes. Please." Leo stands up, holding his hand out to me to help me up. Hand in hand, we carefully walk to the restaurant, ducking in and out of sunbeds and umbrellas so not to be seen.

"Hey!" A security guard has spotted us hiding behind a table.

"Run!" Leo shouts, wrapping his arm around my waist steadying me as we run as fast as we can. Leo pulls me into a storage shed. We squeeze in behind some stacked sunbeds, our bodies pressed together. We watch through a crack in the door as the guard runs straight past us. After a moment, the relief has us laughing. As I make a move to leave now that the coast is clear, Leo pushes me back against the wall with his body. He cups my face with his hands again. His eyes widen.

"Marry me, Kat-er-een."

"Yes," I reply instantly.

We kiss until my lips are numb. When we get back outside, we excitedly plan our future together. We can't get married yet, of course—we are only fifteen, but when we are older, we will. I will move to Italy, open a fancy hair salon, and we will have lots of children. The planning continues late into the night while we stare at the stars. Thankfully, my mum has been having just as much fun with the Italian men as I have with Leo and never questions where I am at any point in the holiday.

The day Mum and I have to return home comes too quickly. My heart breaks, leaving Leo. I have fallen madly in love with him.

"You send letter every week," Leo confirms for about the hundredth time.

"Yes, and we will speak on the phone every day?" I reply.

"Yes. 01264765908." Leo recites my home telephone number back to me, making me smile through my tears. After one last kiss, I brokenheartedly board the coach back to the airport.

It's the longest journey home, each bit of distance travelled making the crack in my heart grow even bigger. When we do return to our home, we are greeted by the phone ringing. I answer it immediately, bursting into tears of joy when I hear Leo's voice.

Every day from then on, Leo calls right on time.

I pull the house phone wire as far as I can so I can sit in the coat cupboard and speak to Leo in private, much to my mum's annoyance. We write to each other once a week, and Leo's English has improved every time we speak.

This afternoon I have signed up to an Italian language class. I can't wait to tell Leo when he calls tonight. But when I arrive home, our front door is locked. Mum never locks the door when we are in, and she often forgets to lock it when she goes out. She wouldn't have locked it knowing I was on my way home.

"Katherine." My mum's voice behind me has me backing away from the door. That's when I notice the signs. Eviction notices. There's one on the door and one on each window. "I'm sorry, sweetheart. There's nothing I can do."

Panic sets in as I hear the house phone ringing inside. I know that will be Leo.

"I need to get in. I need to speak to Leo," I cry.

"We can't, Katherine. Everything has been repossessed," Mum explains sadly.

"But I need my things. I need my letters from Leo. I need to tell him what's happening."

"Come on. I'm dropping you off at your dad's. You can ring Leo from there."

But I couldn't. I couldn't remember his number. Leo always rang me.

The devastation I felt when I lost all contact

with him comes flooding back.

I tried to remember his address, but I couldn't. I tried searching the internet, but there was no Facebook or social media back then. By the time there was, I couldn't remember his surname. But today, seeing it there in front of me in black and white, I know that is his name.

The last letter I wrote to him also comes back to me:

My Leo, of course I will marry you. I promise you, if neither of us is married by the time we get to 30, we will marry each other and we will be together forever, just like we planned.

Well, blow me down; it looks like *he* found me.

He could have called first or, you know, sent me a message on Instagram or something. I am obviously assuming there isn't an actual wedding, and that's just something to grab my attention and make me get on that plane, which I am not doing. I can't.

I'm carrying on with my full set of foils on Mrs. Blackwood when I see one of the guys who were at Jax's house walk past the salon. He looks straight in through the window, making eye contact with me. Chills spread throughout my body, making me feel sick. He didn't see me at the house, so how does he know who I am? Maybe it's just a coincidence. Maybe it's not the guy I saw at

Jax's door. I look at Mike, the security guard who has also spotted the guy looking at me. He walks over to him, but the guy quickly leaves. Mike comes in and quietly speaks to me so the clients can't hear.

"Do you know that man, Katie?"

"No, I don't think so."

"That's the third time he has walked past the salon today. I have radioed down to the hotel door security, and they are escorting him out. He won't be coming back. There's something very unnerving about the way he was acting. If you see him again, Katie, you must tell me. Even if it is outside of work hours, you call me. Understood?"

"Yes. Thanks, Mike."

I am really freaking out now.

I don't know what to do. Should I tell Mike about what has happened with Jax? Mike is a good friend. He would help, but then, I don't know what I would be dragging him into. Plus, I'd hate to get Jax into more trouble. I'm hurt by the way Jax spoke to me on the phone. Ordering me about like I was nothing to him. He didn't once ask me how I was. This is the end for us, I'm sure of it.

I could do with lying low for a while until it all blows over. Maybe I will go to Italy, get away from it all. *No, don't be silly, Katie; you can't just drop everything and go. You have commitments.*

Shaking my head at myself, I carry on highlighting the client's hair in front of me.

On my break, I go into the staffroom and get the wedding invitation out of my bag. I scrutinise it again, but I see nothing new. There's no contact number or address. Just the wedding date and our names.

Looking at the plane ticket, I realise it is for tonight. I look up the flight number online to check if it is real, and it is. This is crazy, but I think I am going to go. It's just a little holiday until things with Jax sort themselves out, I tell myself. It will be nice to catch up with Leo again and see what he has been up to. I hope things are better now with his father. I remember the sadness in his eyes when he used to speak of him.

I talk to Bella, and she gives the go-ahead for some emergency annual leave starting tomorrow. As soon as I finish work, I throw a load of clothes in my little suitcase, quickly change, grab my passport, and get a black cab to the airport.

I find the right check-in desk and hand over my ticket.

"Good evening, Miss Harris. We have a note here to upgrade you on check-in. So you will be seated in row two in first class. As you are flying first class, you have exclusive use of the Galleries First Lounge, where everything is complimentary. The door is to the right. On behalf of British

Airways, I wish you a safe and enjoyable trip. If there's anything we can help you with during your journey with us, please speak to one of our representatives. Have a good evening, Miss Harris."

My mouth is open as I retrieve my boarding pass. I am stunned. Okay, is Leo now rich? I mean, I know we were only teenagers when we met, but he never came across as having money. He was always so scared of being seen in the hotel. Like he wasn't allowed in there because he couldn't afford it. He used to say he didn't belong there, as if his family were from a different class to those staying in the 5-star hotel. It didn't and doesn't matter to me, but this upgrade has shocked me. I was going to offer to pay him back for the flight when I got there, but I'm not sure I'll have enough in my bank for a first-class ticket.

I go into the lounge and take advantage of the complimentary food and wine. I feel a lot more relaxed with a full tummy and a little alcohol running through my veins. We board on time, and I'm soon sat comfortably in my seat.

"Good evening, Miss Harris. Here is the menu for your meal on board the flight tonight. If you'd like to get comfortable, I will return shortly to take your food and drinks order."

Wow, just, wow. Well, I haven't been on a plane like this before. Normally, when I travel, there are three or four seats in the area where my one seat/bed/sofa room is. There's a large reclining leather seat and an electric retractable footrest, so you can pretty much lie down. There's a table beside me that, just like the recliner, moves wherever you like with a touch of a button. I'm going to enjoy this. Shame the flight isn't longer.

I order a filet steak, and it is cooked to perfection. After I've enjoyed a few glasses of champagne, the flight is soon over, and I'm disappointed when I have to leave the plane. However, the bag of complimentary gifts softens the blow.

I collect my suitcase from the carousel and make my way out to arrivals. The alcohol seems to have worn off, and I'm feeling quite nervous now. I am expecting to see Leo waiting for me by the exit. At least, I'm hoping he is, as I haven't got an address to get a taxi to. Oh gosh, what am I doing here? This is madness. I decide that if he's not here in ten minutes, I will book into a hotel nearby. But surely he wouldn't have gone to all this trouble to then leave me alone in Italy.

I search the crowds for someone who looks like a thirty-year-old version of Leo. There are a lot of handsome Italian men, but nobody I recognise. After ten minutes, the crowds have disappeared, and there's no sign of Leo. Trying not to be disheartened, I join the taxi queue outside the airport and google hotels nearby on my phone. I'm feeling a little disappointed after imaging our reunion—Leo and I running into each other's arms, him picking me up and spinning me around. I give myself a stern talking to; this is not some cute romance novel. This is real life.

First of all, it has been a long time since Leo and I saw each other; we won't be picking up where we left off.

Second, who knows what is happening with Jax? Although after our last conversation, I am not sure he has any feelings for me at all, and to be honest, I'm not sure how I really feel about him. We had only been together for six months, and I actually can't see us spending the rest of our lives together. But that conversation should take place with him before starting up anything else.

And third of all, I am in a beautiful country; I want to relax and enjoy it with no drama. I'm supposed to be escaping man trouble, not finding more.

As I approach the end of the taxi queue, a deep voice behind me makes me jump.

"Katherine Harris?"

I turn to see a large Italian man in a black pinstripe suit. But it's not Leo.

Chapter 3

Katie

"Yes, that's me."

"Your transport is over here," the man says in a thick Italian accent as he nods towards a black SUV with blacked-out windows. The other people in the queue look from me to him with concern. I question whether or not to go with him.

He walks towards the vehicle, shouting over his shoulder as he does. "Mr. Guerra does not like to wait!"

He obviously knows Leo, so I decide to go with him. I'll go to meet Leo and catch up; then, I will book a hotel. I am feeling quite on edge. Who does Leo think he is? Come to think of it, it's a bit presumptuous expecting me to come all the way here with not even a phone call. Plus, it's rude not to even pick me up himself. Mr. Guerra doesn't like to wait, does he not? Well, I am going to tell him a few things I don't like when I see him. I'll see him now, thank him for the plane ticket, and then go enjoy my holiday in Italy on my own.

Grunting from the grumpy Italian quickly brings me back to the moment. He reluctantly takes my case and opens the back door for me; I climb in. As I'm still feeling a little tipsy, I decide to kill him with kindness.

"Thank you so much for picking me up, Mr...?"

"Marco."

"Mr. Marco."

"No! Just Marco."

"Okay, 'just' Marco. I'm Katie. It's nice to meet you."

Marco growls and mutters something in Italian under his breath.

"So, where are we going?" I ask while I take in the Italian views whizzing past my window. "Even at night, the scenery is spectacular."

Marco looks at me through this rearview mirror, his eyes frowning.

"I absolutely love Italy. I love the food, the weather, the people. Oh, I can't wait to see Leo. How is Leo? What is he up to these days?" I twitter on.

Marco huffs, annoyed by my chatter. He raises up a privacy screen between us. Charming.

I get my phone out and let my parents and Bella know I have landed safely. They all think

I have taken a holiday to get over my breakup with Jax. They all know I'm in Italy, so at least if I go missing, they will know where to look. *Oh goodness, do not think like that, Katie.* I am perfectly safe. I will meet up with Leo, thank him for his generosity, pay him back, and then do my own thing. My dad will send me more money if needed. I don't like to be in debt to anyone. Well, except my dad, but that's what Dad's are for.

Catching up on my messages and searching for a hotel takes my mind off my current situation. Google has found me lots of hotels with availability. I am waiting to see where we are going before I decide which one to stay in. The nearest hotel to where we end up will be my first choice for tonight. I'm exhausted. A few days there to start with, and then I'll move on. It's not my first time in Italy, but there are still places I haven't seen and many places I want to see again. A little tour around the country is just what the doctor ordered.

The movement of the car changes. Through the window, I see we are driving down a long pebbled driveway. Lights at either side lead us down to a well-lit house. It is a large white building with shutters on either side of the windows and ivy growing up on one side. It looks expensive and very Italian.

Marco collects my case from the boot and leads me into the house. The hallway is bright; it smells floral and clean. It's all marble floors and extravagant paintings and vases. I follow Marco into what looks like a library.

"Sit." Marco points to a leather Chesterfield sofa as he leaves the room and closes the door behind him.

Not feeling like sitting, I walk around the room, taking in its beauty. There are floor-to-ceiling windows which are covered with heavy gold velvet curtains. Oak bookcases line every wall. Each shelf is full of books. Most are in Italian, but there are some in English. There's a range of fiction and non-fiction. A large desk sits centred at the back of the room. I am about to walk over to it when the door opens behind me; I hear two sets of heavy footsteps enter the room.

One set stops behind me to the left and the other stops at my back. I feel the heat from their body against mine. Their head leans in over my shoulder. Their breath on my ear sends shivers down my spine. I should move, turn around to see who is making my skin prickle with their presence. But I don't. My nose then fills with a scent that makes me breathe in even deeper. I close my eyes, savouring the masculine spice. A light touch of a finger on my ear makes me open them again. The finger traces the edge of my ear from my lobe to the top, finishing by tucking strands of my hair behind it.

"La mia ragazza. You have been hiding from me."

The voice covers my skin in goosebumps. Leaving me frozen to the spot, he continues past me and round the desk at the end of the room.

This man is just as tall as Marco—around six feet. Not built as big but extremely well-built all the same. An expensive suit fits perfectly around each curve of his body. He throws some folders angrily onto his desk. Leaning forward with both hands on the work surface, he slowly raises his head to look at me.

As soon as my eyes land on him, I instantly recognise him as Leo. His expression is cold and devil-like as his eyes roam my body from my feet to my head. When our eyes meet, this, however, instantly changes. His eyes are warm and smiling, even though the rest of his facial expression doesn't match. Feelings flood back to me. Our time together pops freshly back into my memory. Laughing together, teaching each other our languages, walking along the sea, holding hands, kissing…. My tummy flutters with the reminders.

He's so different now, though. He's older, obviously, but he oozes power. He is incredibly attractive. Dark chocolate-brown eyes. Thick black hair. A short black beard perfectly framing his chiselled jawline.

I walk towards him.

"Leo, I—"

A strong hand grips my shoulder, stopping me from moving any further. I wince at the tightness of his hand and try to move away.

Leo abruptly stands tall. His eyes leave mine, and the cold anger returns. "Marco!"

The hand instantly releases its grip. Leo stares at Marco behind me for a few more seconds, his nostrils flaring and his fists clenched at his sides.

When Leo's eyes return to mine, the warmth has gone. Although they're not as cold as they were when he looked at Marco, I do not recognise this man. I need to get out of here.

"Well, it was nice to see you again, Leo, but I really must be going now. I have a hotel reservation, and I am feeling rather tired. Thank you so much for your generosity; I will, of course, pay you back for the flight. Maybe we could meet up for a drink while I am here and catch up…," I continue nervously, making excuses to leave, feeling rather flustered. I move closer to the door. This is the most surreal experience of my life.

A slight smirk appears on one side of Leo's mouth; there's also amusement in his eyes. "Portala nella mia stanza. Non toccarla più!" *Take her to my room. Do not touch her again,* Leo instructs Marco.

"Follow me. I will take you to your accommodation." Marco picks up my case and disappears through the door.

"Oh no, Leo, I don't want to impose. I have a hotel; we can meet up tomorrow or the next day, maybe?"

Leo opens a safe behind a wall in the bookcase. He removes something and tucks it in the inside pocket of his suit jacket and locks the safe. Without looking at me, he walks out of the room as he says, "You will stay with me, Katherine. We will talk tomorrow."

He disappears, leaving me tingling from the way he says my name in his smooth Italian accent. "Kat-er-een." It does the same to me now, all these years later, as it did back then. I feel like a teenager again. Knowing he won't take no for an answer combined with the fact that I don't actually have anywhere to stay, I decide one night won't do any harm. I am shattered and also quite intrigued by my now grumpy and incredibly handsome teenage heartthrob.

I take a few seconds to compose myself before I follow the sound of my name being bellowed down the hallway.

"Miss Harris!"

"Coming, just Marco." I practically run to keep up with him.

Marco shows me to a huge bedroom with thick carpets. The room is very grey. It's nice, don't get me wrong, but very masculine. I take off my shoes and explore as Marco puts my case on the bed and leaves.

"Thanks, just Marco," I tease as he closes the door.

"Sciocca," Marco ironically calls me. *Fool.*

They all assume I do not understand their language. Unbeknown to them, I have a PLIDA certificate, which is basically a certification of competence in the Italian language; I'm fluent.

This is going to be fun.

I fall asleep as soon as my head hits the pillow. The mixture of stress from the last few days and the alcohol I consumed on my journey knocked me straight out. I wake up bursting for the loo.

Sitting on the toilet, I put my head in my hands.

"What am I doing?" I mutter to myself. The reality of the situation hits me like a ton of bricks. I am in a foreign country in a stranger's house, and nobody knows where I am.

"Good morning, Katherine." My stomach drops. The voice is coming from someone also in the bathroom. I slowly look up, scared as to what I will see. And there's Leo in the bathtub, completely naked, with an amused smirk across his face. I quickly wipe, flush, and get the hell out of there.

Leo

I return home at 6:00 a.m., having eradicated one of my problems. My head pounds with the stress and responsibility my lifestyle brings. How is it I erase one complication only to find another has appeared in its place? A prime example of this is currently lying sleeping in my bed. Her blonde hair, tinged with pink, is fanned across my pillow. She's curled up on her side with her flawless, smooth-skinned long legs crossed over each other. Her arms are wrapped around something. I am not sure what it is. Is that a teddy? I stand there and take her in for a moment. She looks like an angel brightening up my dark grey bed. She was supposed to be the means to an end. But now I think she may be the beginning of something I hadn't bargained for.

I remove my blood-stained clothes and run myself a bath, needing to soak off the night's drama and clear my head.

Closing my eyes, I let the warmth of the water soothe my aching muscles. The image of Katherine appears prominently in my mind. When I saw her, I thought I would feel the pain and hate for her that has tormented me for years. That her deceit and betrayal would fuel the plans I have for her. I was not prepared for the comfort I felt when I looked into her eyes. When Marco put his hand on her shoulder, it took all my strength not to pull my gun out from under my desk and put a bullet in my number one's head.

The sound of the bathroom door opening disturbs me from my thoughts. A very sleepy-looking Katherine hurries in and takes a seat on the toilet. Completely oblivious to my presence, she puts her head in her hands and mumbles something to herself. I smile at the sight of her. She always amused me with her little quirks.

"Good morning, Katherine."

She takes a few seconds to look at me, but when she does, her face is a picture. I chuckle at the mortified look and watch her exit my bathroom at a record pace.

With a towel wrapped around me, I go to my wardrobe and pull out some clothes. Katherine watches me, clearly in shock at my brazen actions.

"Leo? What is going on? You said I could use this room, and then you come in unannounced, use my bathroom, and walk around in next to nothing? I need you to speak to me, Leo. What is going on?"

Without saying a word, I drop my towel and begin to get dressed with my back to Katherine.

Gasping she shouts, "What the?! Leo!"

I'm hit on the back with a pillow; I hear her stomping about. The bathroom door slams. She's mad. I like it.

Once I am dressed, I unlock the bathroom door from my side and stand at the sink mirror to do my hair. I try not to look at her naked body behind me.

"Ahh, Seriously! Leo, I am in the shower!"

I ignore her outburst.

"To answer your questions, this is now 'our' room. We will, from now on, be living together and sharing a room."

"What?! No, don't be ridiculous. Why would I do that?"

"Because, Katherine, soon you will be my wife." I walk out of the bathroom and close the door, leaving Katherine shouting obscenities and slamming the shower door.

Chapter 4

Leo

I join Marco in the sitting room. One of the housekeepers pours us both coffee while Marco goes over the distribution restructure now that our little whistle-blower has been erased. We are disturbed from our discussion by the door swinging open.

"Leo. Thank you so much for your hospitality. I will repay you for the flights, but I must go now. It was great to see you again. Goodbye."

Katherine leaves the room, swinging her hips and pulling her little case behind her.

Marco raises his eyebrow at me, no doubt at the fact that I'm wearing an amused smirk, which he definitely doesn't see very often. We both sit in silence, listening to her try to open the front door. The annoyed chatter coming from her makes me bark a laugh. Marco shakes his head at me.

"Leo, I can't seem to open the door. Could you let me out, please?"

"No," I calmy reply, intrigued to see how she reacts.

"What do you mean, no? You can't keep me here! Who the hell do you think you are? Let me go, or I will ring the police!"

Marco stands up, grunting in annoyance. No one would ever disrespect me by speaking to me the way Katherine is. No one would ever dare call me Leo. People have lost their lives for less. She will learn her place in time.

"Take a seat, Katherine." I point to a chair at my side.

Eventually, she reluctantly sits down.

"I have recently taken over my father's business," I begin. "It seems to continue my reign."

Katherine snorts a laugh. "Sorry, your reign? Seriously Leo, what are you, the King of Italy?"

"Questo è esattamente ciò che è." *That is exactly what he is*, Marco states from behind me.

Katherine's eyes dart towards him.

"Stai zitto!" *Be quiet!* I glare at Marco for good measure.

"As I was saying. To ensure I fill my role adequately, I need a wife. And seeing as you so kindly offered, I have decided to take you up on it."

"What offer? When have I ever said I would marry you? You can't seriously be talking about a letter I wrote to you at fifteen years old?"

"You were actually sixteen at that time, and yes. A handwritten and signed agreement."

"Well, I have changed my mind. I don't even know you, Leo."

Although I knew this would be her reaction, I feel a tingle of annoyance.

"I am afraid you don't have any other option, Katherine. I have taken the liberty of arranging a lawyer for you to go through the proposal. This lawyer is completely independent; we had not met until yesterday. I have paid his fees, but he works for you."

I call out, "Agla?!"

Alga, my housekeeper, appears at the sitting-room door.

"Send in Mr. Brooks."

Katie

This cannot be happening; he cannot be serious. A grey-haired gentleman sheepishly enters the room. He greets Leo and Marco without making eye contact.

"We will leave you to discuss matters in private." Leo says, he and Marco then leave the room, closing the door behind them.

Mr. Brooks takes a seat beside me and pulls some documents out of his briefcase.

"He can't be serious, can he?"

"Oh, Miss Harris. I am afraid Mr. Guerra is always serious."

"Okay, so how do I get out of this?"

"I can assure you, Miss Harris—"

"Please call me Katie."

"I have been instructed to only address you as Miss Harris and to stay at least four feet away from you at all times." Mr. Brooks looks at the space between us, obviously calculating the distance. He shuffles his chair further away from mine.

I decide to ignore his comments, keep calm, and encourage him to continue.

"You were saying, Mr. Brooks?"

"Yes, I can assure you I have been through this contract with a fine-tooth comb, and I cannot find a way out. Believe me, Miss, I have tried. I do not agree with what he is doing. Unfortunately, though, in this country, a handwritten signed document written by anyone aged sixteen or over is a law-binding agreement. For any breach of the contract, Mr. Guerra can take legal action. Although considering who Mr. Guerra is, I don't think 'legal' action would be the road he takes."

"What do you mean, 'who' Mr. Guerra is?"

Mr. Brooks hands me some papers.

"You need to read these. Contact numbers are at the bottom of the page if you have any questions. My advice to you, Miss Harris, is to keep your head down and try to find a way to convince Mr. Guerra to cancel the proposal himself."

As if Leo has been listening to the conversation, he enters the room.

"I will see you out, Mr. Brooks."

Left in the room on my own, I look at the papers in my hand. "Marriage Contract" is the title of the first sheet. It has lists of what will be expected of "Mrs. Guerra."

1.   As the wife of Leonardo Guerra, it is not necessary for you to work. All your needs will be provided for.

2.   As part of the Guerra family, you will be expected to keep to a healthy diet and exercise regime. Training will be arranged at convenient times by Mr. Guerra.

3.   The Guerra has a reputation to uphold; you must always look your uttermost best.

4.   You will be expected to be available to Mr. Guerra at all times.

5.   You will attend events and must always stay at Mr. Guerra's side.

6.   As his wife you will obey and respect every decision he makes.

And the list goes on and on. At the bottom, it states:

Failure to adhere to any of these points will be a violation of the marriage contract and, therefore, will result in legal action.

I feel like I am being set up. This is a prank; it's got to be. Someone is going to jump out from behind the curtains with a TV camera, shouting, "Gotcha!"

I stare at the papers in disbelief. *Okay, Katie, do not panic.* As I flick through the pile, I feel some sheets at the back which are a different size to all the rest. When I pull them out, I recognise the handwritten letters. They're my letters. He kept them all this time.

I need to speak to Leo.

I find him in the hallway speaking in Italian to Marco.

"Lei è una responsabilità!" *She is a liability!*

"Stai mettendo in discussione il mio giudizio?" *Are you questioning my judgement?*

Good, so Marco obviously doesn't think this whole charade is a good idea either.

"Leo? Can I have a moment of your time, please?"

Leo slowly turns to me, scowling at my interruption.

"My time, Katherine, is a privilege. You have yet to earn your privileges."

Flabbergasted, I stare at him, open-mouthed. I have no words. So I change the subject. "Does this wonderful house have a swimming pool?"

Both men look at me like I have said something ridiculous.

"Yes." Leo replies sternly.

"Well, where is it?" I ask, trying to sound unaffected by what has just happened.

Marco looks at me furiously.

"At the back of the house." Leo gestures down the hallway.

"Good, well, if I am stuck here, I may as well make use of the place. I am on holiday, after all. My tan needs a top-up. Have a good day, boys. If you need me, I'll be sunning myself by the pool. Arrivederci!" *Bye-bye.*

Oops, I need to be careful not to use Italian around them. I doubt they will think I know more than that, though. Everyone knows how to say hello and goodbye in different languages, don't they?

The bedroom I'm staying in is huge. Finding

an empty wardrobe and some drawers, I unpack my things. I decide the best thing to do is stay calm and play dumb about the situation. I need to carefully find out all I can about Leo, his life, and why he chose me for an arranged marriage. Marco doesn't want me here, and Leo seems easy to wind up. So a little fun along the way won't go amiss either.

Now that I've changed into my bikini, I look at myself in the mirror. Fitness is what keeps me sane, so I am pretty toned. I must find out if there's a gym here; given the size of this house, I bet there is. My boobs are huge, and this bikini I got last year doesn't do much to cover them. Oh well. I throw on a beach dress, then grab my bag, Kindle, towel, and sun cream and go look for the pool.

Walking through the house, I see the kitchen. The smell of fresh bread draws me in. I see a man in a traditional chef uniform mixing something in a bowl; he looks up to greet me.

"Buongiorno!" His bright, smiling face instantly puts me at ease.

"Good morning," I reply, appreciating the warm welcome.

"Come, come. Let me make you some breakfast."

"Some coffee would be great, thank you."

"No, no, no." He tuts and shakes his head.

I take a seat at the island and watch him arrange pastries and fruit on a tray.

"Alga will serve you in the dining room." The chef nods to the door where a middle-aged lady stands with a pleasant smile.

"If it's okay with you, I'll just sit here?"

The chef looks at Alga, then back at me, a confused look on his face. Alga comes and stands at his side and gently pats his arm.

Alga nods and smiles at me. "Of course." She pours me some coffee.

"I'm Katie, by the way."

"Alga, and this is my husband, Sergio."

I knew it. They both have the same kind and caring aura about them. I eat my breakfast while making small talk about the weather and how beautiful the house and gardens are. From my seat at the island, I can see out into the back. A large stone patio leads out onto a landscaped garden surrounded by Mediterranean flowers. There are different levels to the gardens, one with a beautiful fountain and another with a pool that has a waterfall. I'm excited about getting out there. Once I finish my breakfast, I pick up my cup and plate to take it over to the sink. Alga dashes towards me in a panic.

"No, miss. I will take that for you."

Just as I'm about to protest, I see the

pleading look in her eyes. I glance over her shoulder to see Marco standing at the door, watching our every move. I let Alga take them from me and gather up my things.

"Thank you so much for breakfast, both of you; it was lovely to meet you, Alga, Sergio. I'll see you later on." I squeeze past Marco in the doorway, making my way outside.

"Katie!" Alga shouts after me, waving a bottle of water in her hand. "Please, take this. It is very hot out there today."

"Thank you, Alga." Marco snatches the bottle from her before I can reach for it.

So I snatch it from him in the same way. His eyes bulge in fury. I give him a sarcastic smile and continue outside. The warm air hits me as soon as I open the door. Beautiful smells tingle my nose. Fresh warm air, flowers, trees, the sea? We must be close to the beach. Wonderful.

I find a sun lounger near the pool and set my towel down. I take off my dress and start applying my sun cream. A loud smash draws my attention back to the house. I see Marco in the kitchen, waving his hands about. He looks angry. What is his problem? Deciding I need to cause a distraction, I take off my bikini top and carry on applying my cream.

"Boss!" I hear Marco bellow through the house, followed by shouted obscenities in Italian.

I put on my sunglasses and sit back on the lounger to watch the situation unfold. I see a few men start to appear at the windows of the house. Leo arrives in the kitchen. Marco shouts something and points to me outside. Leo stands frozen on the spot for a moment until Marco shouts again. The door to the house swings open with such force, it bangs into a plant to the side of it, breaking the window and shattering the glass across the patio.

"Kat-er-een!"

I remove my sunglasses and put on my most innocent face.

Chapter 5

Katie

"Oh, hi, Leo. Are you coming to join me?"

His nostrils flare. "What the hell are you doing?"

"I'm sunbathing, silly. Hey, while you're here, will you put some cream on my back?" I climb off the lounger and stand facing the house. I hear a few whistles and male chatter coming from within.

"Cover yourself immediately!" Leo stands in front of me, shielding my body from the view of the house. His face is red, with beads of sweat appearing on his forehead.

"How can I get a tan if I am all covered up?"

"Sunbathing is over." He removes his shirt and puts it around me.

Mesmerised by his tanned, chiselled chest, I let him dress me. Taking my hand, he pulls me to the house. My hand feels so small in his. Stopping on the patio, he notices the broken glass and my lack of footwear. Leo picks me up in one quick scoop, as if I'm light as a feather. Marco is standing at the door. He moves at the last second to let us pass. His face is full of annoyance at the sight of us. I give him a cheesy smile and wink as we go past him. Leo carries me to the bedroom and throws me onto the bed.

"Why do you disrespect me?" Leo stands at the foot of the bed with his dark, angry eyes upon me. "You belong to me now."

"I belong to no one," I spit back at him.

Leo dives onto the bed, his body on top of mine, legs on either side of my hips, elbows on either side of my head.

He whispers in my ear, "You belong to me. You always have, and you always will. You just don't know it yet. But you will learn. Every. Little. Part of you—" He licks the edge of my ear with the tip of his tongue. "—belongs to only me. Mine to look at. Mine to touch. Mine to taste."

"Don't you touch me!" I push him off me, and to my surprise, he gets up.

"I will only touch you when you beg me to."

"Ha, that will never happen."

"We will see. Now get dressed. I am taking you out."

I put on a summer dress and some comfortable wedge sandals. A bit of light makeup and a wave in my hair will have to do. Leo exits the bathroom, once again wearing in his usual suit. He frowns as he takes me in.

"What? At least I am dressed for the weather. Don't you get a little hot, always wearing a suit?"

"Let's go." He ignores my statement and leaves the room. I follow him out to the front of the house.

"Questa non è una buona idea!" *This is not a good idea!* shouts Marco as Leo opens the car door for me to get in.

Leo ignores him. He starts the engine and drives away at top speed.

The car is a classic convertible. My hair blows in the wind as we drive. I hadn't noticed in the dark on the way here, but the house is surrounded by a large vineyard.

"Wow, is this all yours, Leo?" I'm impressed.

"Yes. We grow grapes and lemons."

We exit the grounds and turn onto a road that runs along the cliff edge. The view of the sea is spectacular. After about five minutes, we pull into a building at the side of the road. Leo opens my door and leads me up a stone staircase. At the top is a very traditional Italian restaurant with views looking out to the sea. The restaurant looks very busy; all the tables are full.

"Signor Guerra, mi scuso per favore—due minuti." *Mr. Guerra, apologies, please—two minutes.* The waiter looks panicked.

Leo checks his phone. I watch the waiter. He approaches a couple eating at a table overlooking the sea. Speaking to them with his head down, he clears their plates while they are still eating. The man stands up, saying something to the waiter and looks, quite rightly, very annoyed. The waiter gestures towards Leo. After a quick glance our way, the couple both help clear the table. *What on earth?* Once the table is cleared and reset, the waiter calls us over.

"You do realise the waiter made a couple move halfway through eating so we could sit here?" I mention as we sit down.

Leo shrugs. "This is where I like to sit. He will have moved them to another table."

"No, he didn't. There are no other tables available. They are standing up at the bar, eating their soup."

Leo doesn't look in their direction. He just stares at me quizzically.

"What would you like to drink, Katherine?"

"Prosecco would be nice."

"Good choice."

The waiter appears, and Leo orders our drinks. I have so much I want to say to him, to ask him, but I do not know where to start. So I just sit in silence, taking in the view while sipping my drink.

The prosecco is delicious. Crisp, fruity, and cold. Leo stares at me intently, watching me drink every sip.

"You make this, don't you?"

"Yes. Well, not me personally, but that is a Guerra Prosecco," he answers proudly.

The waiter puts some plates down in front of us.

"What is this?" I stare at the plate in front of me.

"Burrata al Tartufo. It's a mozzarella cheese with mushrooms and truffles."

"I can order my own food, Leo. Do I not even get to choose what I eat now?"

Leo smirks at me and offers me the menu. Damn. It's all in Italian, which is fine because I understand Italian, but I don't want him to know that yet.

I think back to when we met. We would spend our days together teaching each other our languages. It's ignorant of him to think that I would not continue to learn his language while he has learnt mine so fluently. Leo definitely taught me how to say pollo, which is chicken. I would always sneak chicken nuggets out of the restaurant for us to eat together. It looks like I am having the chicken, then, annoyingly. I would much prefer one of the fish dishes.

"I'll have the pollo," I say, putting down my menu.

Leo stifles a laugh.

The chicken is actually delicious, and I have polished off another two glasses of prosecco. Having swallowed a little Dutch courage, I decide now is the time to question Leo.

"So why me, Leo, out of all the women in the world?"

"Why not you?" Leo's phone rings. He answers it when he sees the caller ID.

"Si?" *Yes?* "Come è successo di nuovo!?" *How has this happened again!?* "Impostare una riunione." *Set up a meeting.* He ends the call and stands up. "We are leaving."

On the journey home, Leo is very distracted, but I press for more answers.

"When is 'our' wedding, then?"

"In two months."

That surprises me; it's not as soon as I would have thought, which is good—it buys me some time. "My father has some medical treatments in a couple of weeks, which puts him out for a while. By then, he will be strong enough to attend the ceremony."

The car is speeding through the narrow streets. I hold on to the seat to stop myself from being thrown into the side of the door. Leo looks tense.

"Is everything okay?"

"What?" he barks, not taking his eyes off the road.

"Is everything okay? The phone call at the restaurant—was it bad news?"

"No, everything is not okay!" Leo puts his foot down even further, throwing me back into my seat.

Going the speed we are, returning to the house doesn't take long. He pulls to a quick stop at the front steps. He quickly rounds the car and flings my door open, not waiting for me to exit; he rushes into the house, shouting for Marco.

Back in my room, I get out the contract and read through it again, still in disbelief.

Number 7 on the list of what is expected of "Mrs. Guerra."

7. The Guerra family must continue their bloodline therefore, a minimum of four children are expected to be born in the first six years of marriage. Two of these children must be male.

This can't be legal. Surely, I cannot be forced into this.

I decide to ring Damien, my friend Bella's husband. He owns a security and protection company and has dealt with many difficult situations. If anyone can get me out of this mess, Damien can. He answers on the first ring. Listening intently, he doesn't say a word until I have told him every detail.

"Okay, Katie. Send me copies of everything you have been given. Coincidently, I know of Leonardo Guerra. He is a distant relative, although I don't know him well. The Guerras are a powerful family, Katie. However, I don't think you are currently in any immediate danger. But you need to be careful. Try to keep the Katie cheekiness to a minimum. I will contact my solicitor, Mr. Davies, as soon as we end this call. Try not to panic; just give me some time."

Although I am a little disappointed Damien didn't say how ludicrous this all was, that there's no way he can force me to do this, I do trust Damien and have faith that he will sort this out for me. I google Leonardo Guerra and the Guerra family, but all that comes up is their wine business. I'm not an idiot; I know there's more to Leo. Trust me to promise marriage to the Italian Devil.

Putting all negative thoughts to the back of

my mind, I take myself on a tour of the house. It's a beautiful modern Italian house. There are many different hallways; I lose my bearings a few times. After having a nosey around the gym, which I will be using, the library, and numerous sitting rooms. I hear voices coming from behind a bookcase. I quickly hide in the room opposite and watch through the crack in the door. I'm mesmerised as the bookcase moves out and to the side, making way for Leo, Marco, and two other guys I don't recognise. Well, now I am intrigued. I need to find out what is through that secret door. Unfortunately, the bookcase quickly returns to its place not long after the men disappear.

I burn some energy off in the gym. When I've finished my intense workout, my gym shorts and bra are soaked and stuck to my skin. Having had my earphones in, I'm startled to see Leo in the corner, watching me.

"Oh, you made me jump. How long have you been standing there?"

"Long enough. I will always find you now, Kat-er-een. You cannot hide from me again."

"I wasn't hiding."

Goose bumps spread across my body in the wake of his gaze.

"We are going out tonight. Have you got something sensible to wear?" His tone is sarcastic as his eyes roam my body.

"Well, that depends on what you mean by sensible."

"I will find you something to wear." He straightens from his leaning position against the wall.

"That won't be necessary. I have plenty of clothes. Where are we going anyway?"

"To dinner with my family. Wear something decent... and underwear." He glares at my nipples protruding through my sports bra before he turns and closes the door. The noise echoes throughout the gym.

On my way back to my room, I decide to check out the bookcase; it's been on my mind throughout my workout. After pulling on a few books that don't move, I find one that gives way to reveal a number panel. It doesn't move an inch with my pushing and pulling, so I give up. Deep male voices coming down the hall have my heart racing. I quickly return to my previous hiding spot opposite. In the rush, I haven't returned the book to its position covering the control panel. Panic sets in. I hold my breath and watch.

Chapter 6

Katie

The two guys from earlier return—no Leo or Marco. The panel on show doesn't seem to faze them. One of them types in the code. 2-0-0...? Damn. His hand hid the last number. There are only ten possibilities, though, I suppose. After they enter, I swiftly return to my room.

Once I'm ready, I find Leo sitting in the outside dining area with Marco.

They're both drinking a beer.

"Katie, can I get you—"

Leo interrupts Alga. "It's Katherine, not Katie!"

"Katie or Katherine is fine by me, Alga." I smile apologetically at her.

"What can I get you to drink?"

"I'm not sure. Can I come with you and take a look?"

Alga looks to Leo, and so do I. Without

taking his eyes off me, he nods. I follow Alga to the bar area, giving Marco a big smile as I do. He doesn't like me one bit. The feeling is mutual.

"Is he always this grumpy?"

"Si, he has a lot on his shoulders."

I find a bottle of gin I like; Alga passes me a glass with ice and some tonic. I make myself a strong one.

"Do you know why I am here, Alga?"

"Si, you are Mr. Guerra's fiancée."

"Do you know I haven't seen or heard from Leo for fifteen years?"

"I do not know all the details. I have only been told to treat you as a Guerra. Deep down, he is a good boy. Spero che tu possa salvarlo." *I hope you can save him.*

"I'm not sure about that." I look at her, and her eyes widen.

"Sei più intelligente di quanto lasci intendere," she says. *You are smarter than you let on.* "Le cose non sono sempre come sembrano." *Things are not always what they seem.*

With a little squeeze of my hand, she ushers me back outside to the guys. I know my secret is safe with her.

It is a beautiful evening. It is still very warm, even though the sun is getting ready to set. The sky is a beautiful shade of pink. Leo and Marco are talking about cars, so I take a walk around the garden, feeling Leo's eyes follow me as I do.

"Time to go." Leo shouts, beckoning me towards him.

Marco enters the house while Leo waits for me to approach.

"How do I look?" I do a little spin, letting my white sun dress float up slightly around me.

"Like mine," he groans, making me feel a little lightheaded.

I ignore it.

"I mean my dress. Will it do?"

"Yes, it will do. But this little pirouette you just did. You only do that for me. Understand?" A small smirk appears on his face.

Holding the door open for me, he places his hand on the small of my back and leads me through the house and out of the front to the waiting cars.

It's a short, scenic drive from Leo's house.

It's a garden party—or rather, a field party. We are at Leo's parent's house, and it is even more luxurious than his. The event is a grand affair with marquees filled with finely dressed tables, waiters and waitresses walking around with silver trays, cosy seating areas with firepits, and the whole place is lit up with fairy lights.

"Come, let me introduce you to my parents." With a light hand on my back, Leo leads me to a well-dressed couple.

"Papà, Mamma, I would like to introduce Katherine."

His father glares at me as if my presence annoys him. I feel extremely unwelcome.

"Stai ancora continuando con questo?" *You are still continuing with this?*

Leo stands tall, and I sense his frustration. In a swift motion, Leo takes two glasses of wine from a passing waiter and hands one each to his mother and me.

"I need to speak to my father. You stay here."

Mrs. Guerra is thankfully much more welcoming and, to my surprise—English.

"It's lovely to meet you, Mrs. Guerra. You have a very beautiful home."

"Thank you. I am pleased to meet you, too, Katherine. I have heard little about you, but you have obviously made a big impression on my son. Tell me—quickly, before the men return—how did you two meet?"

Putting her arm through mine, she leads us to a quieter area of the party. Although friendly enough, Mrs. Guerra oozes power. I feel I have no other option but to tell her the truth, the whole truth, and nothing but the truth—so I do.

After telling Mrs. Guerra all about our whirlwind romance when we were teenagers, and how I had heartbreakingly lost contact with him, Mrs. Guerra seems very concerned.

"I see, and does my son know why you lost contact all those years ago?"

"No. I don't suppose he does. We haven't spoken about it. We have spoken very little since I got here, to be honest."

"Mrs. Guerra, Mrs. Guerra!" We both turn towards the shouting.

A woman who is of a similar age to Mrs. Guerra pulls her into a hug. I can't help but notice how Mrs. Guerra's body language changes. Her back becomes straighter, and although she is smiling, it's not the welcoming smile I received. Another woman about my age appears beside them. Both women are extremely beautiful. Long dark, shimmering hair, big brown eyes, each of them perfectly immaculate.

"Ladies, I would like you to meet Katherine, Leo's fiancée."

This is so surreal. I feel a little off-balance at the title. Mrs. Guerra links her arm with mine.

"Fiancée?" the older lady says, appearing mortified.

"Since when?" the lady about my age inquires. "Isn't this all a little rushed?"

"Not at all; in fact, Katherine was just this minute telling me how she and Leo met when they were teenagers, many years ago. Young love—it really is quite romantic."

"Special? But no ring?" The older woman eyeballs my ring finger.

"Leo has found nothing quite special enough just yet, but he will; plus, Katherine isn't a materialist like some people I know." Mrs. Guerra gives both ladies a big smile. "If you'll excuse us, we have very important people to speak to."

We move to a seating area and are brought fresh drinks and canapes.

"Promise me, Katherine. As soon as you get the chance, speak to Leo about what happened with your mother and how you lost touch."

"I will. I promise."

"You remind me a little of myself, Katherine."

And that's all she says on the matter as we are joined again by Leo and his father. His parents dismiss themselves, leaving us alone.

"You know, Leo, you didn't have to force me to marry you to get me here. I would have jumped at the chance to meet up with you again."

Leo huffs a sarcastic laugh. I ignore him and continue.

"For years, I hoped we would bump into each other. I looked online for you a few years ago, but I found nothing."

Leo raises his eyebrow, looking at me more intensely but not saying a word.

"I have thought about you a lot. Even dreamt about you."

Leo stands up. "Enough talking. We have people we must speak to." He holds out his hand to help me up, I take it and decide to try and discuss it again later.

I'm introduced to many people. Leo tries to keep the conversations in English, but they quickly turn to Italian. Most of it is boring small talk or business, but I have found out a few interesting facts. There's something big happening tomorrow night that Leo wants to take the lead on, and the two ladies I met while with Mrs. Guerra are the mother and daughter of Leo's father's business partner. Although they all interact in a friendly enough way, I sense there is some animosity between them.

It's late when we return to the house. I had hoped I could finish our conversation, but Leo insists on being on his own and retires to his office. I get into bed, but my mind is in overdrive. I need to understand what is going on. I will let Leo have tonight, but tomorrow, I will insist he speaks to me and explains.

Chapter 7

Leo

Katherine's excuses tonight have me thinking of the past. The painful memories I have chosen not to think about return to my mind in full force. The heartache and desperation I felt as a teenager when my contact with Katherine suddenly ended. She was my escape, my sense of calm that made my troubled life bearable. After months of unanswered letters and calls, I thought the worst had happened.

It took me years to find her, but with the help of an investigator at age eighteen, I found an address. I immediately travelled to England to find her. I knocked on the door of the address with my heart pounding. When there was no answer, a neighbour asked if she could help me. I explained that I was looking for Katherine. She told me there was no Katherine living there, only a Katie and a Paul.

"Here they come now." The lady pointed to a couple walking arm in arm down the street.

It was her. The realisation hit me hard. My Katherine had moved on.

She was living with another man and changed her name to stop me from finding her.

My heart completely broke.

I left before she saw me and threw up in someone's front garden.

When I returned home, my life and family were in a state of war.

My older brother had been executed. He had been fed to the wolves by his fiancée. The person he loved and trusted the most had cruelly deceived him. Unbeknown to him, he had fallen in love with the daughter of my father's biggest rival. After much disagreement, the fathers eventually held a truce so they could be together. But it was all a trick—a plan to break our family.

The night it happened, I was supposed to be with my brother. I should have been there to protect him. Things may have turned out very differently if I had been. But I was not there; I was in England, searching for a woman who had betrayed me. That was the moment I realised women were never to be trusted. They are liars and cheats.

Fury builds inside me. I throw the bottle of scotch I am holding against the wall of my office.

I was not meant for this life. My brother was

supposed to take over from my father, not me.

Marco appears at the door.

"Esci cazzo!" *Get the fuck out!* I spit.

Marco is my cousin, friend, and underboss. He has been by my side since my brother passed. Guiding and training me, turning me into the Don I need to be. Unlike my brother, who was born to reign, I have had to fight against my natural instincts to become who I am today. But I will not let our legacy down. Our family has suffered enough. It is my duty.

It feels like whatever I do just isn't good enough. Long-standing deals are being abolished. Trades and deliveries are being intercepted. Men are going rogue in their duties. There is a weak link somewhere that, for the life of me, I cannot find.

Father thinks I need to earn more respect. He has insisted I marry, start a family, and continue the legacy. It is the last thing I want. I do not trust women.

If I were to marry, it needs to be someone I can control. The life they'll lead will not be a kind one—not with me. What woman would want that burden? There is only one woman I wish a life of pain on—the woman who promised me a life together and then took it away. I am about to make Katherine redeem that debt. To take what I am owed.

I drink until I can no longer stand.

Katie

Still unable to sleep, I hear the bedroom door open. It's Leo. He wobbles in, mumbling something to himself. Undressing, he stumbles, clearly extremely drunk. I almost get up to help him, but I don't want him to know I am awake. The room is dark, but I can just about make out the muscular shape of his body in the moonlight. When down to his underwear, he climbs into bed and lies by my side. I lie still and close my eyes. I feel him looking at me.

"La mia ragazza," he whispers before turning onto his back and drifting off to sleep. *My girl.*

With even less chance of going to sleep now, I decide to make myself a drink. I get out of bed quietly and leave the room. On my way to the kitchen, I hear muffled voices. I follow the sound to Leo's office. I put my ear to the door.

"Lei non è un problema." *She is not a problem.*

"Lei è già un problema, Marco!" *She is already a problem, Marco!*

I hear heels clicking against the floor, so I dash to the kitchen just as the door opens. I watch

Marco escort out the woman I met this evening, the daughter of Mr. Guerra's senior business partner. Mia, her name is, if I remember rightly. I wonder if Leo knows she is here. Marco kicks the door in temper as she leaves; this makes me jump, a gasp escaping my mouth. Marco turns to see me in the kitchen.

"What the hell are you doing creeping around at this time?" he snaps.

"I wasn't creeping. I've come to make a drink."

"Well, make one!"

Jeez, he is so abrupt.

He disappears into the house, leaving me to it. I warm some milk in the microwave and make a milky coffee. Settling in the lounge with my teddy, I go through my phone. I have a missed call from an unknown number. Thinking it may be Damien, I make a mental note to ring him in the morning. Hopefully, he has found a way out of this situation. It's a shame, as I have dreamt about meeting up with Leo for years. But this ultimatum is too much. He is crazy. This is not a life I want to be part of.

Scrolling through my social media, I get homesick. I hope Damien has some good news for me tomorrow. Eventually, I must fall asleep, as I'm woken by Alga.

"Miss Katherine. I'm sorry to wake you. Are

you all right?"

"Sorry, Alga. I'm fine." I yawn and get up, wrapping a blanket Alga must have placed on me around my shoulders.

"Would you like some coffee?"

"I'd love some, thank you."

Sitting in the kitchen, I drink my coffee, enjoying chatting with Alga and Sergio. Sergio is prepping the food for the day, and Alga is cleaning and writing the shopping list. The mood changes when Leo enters.

"Get dressed; we are going out for the day."

"Where are we going?"

"Out."

I roll my eyes at him.

"Fine." With one last sip of my coffee, I jump off the bar stool I'm sitting on and go to my room.

A blacked-out SUV waits for us at the front. Leo opens the door to the back and slides in after me. Marco is in the driver's seat.

I sigh.

"What?" Leo demands after my irritated expression.

"Nothing. Good to see you, just Marco."

Marco ignores me.

We stop in a little town. Its beautiful old

buildings with quaint shops have me smiling from ear to ear. I wander excitedly in and out of each one I pass. Leo tries to keep up, and Marco moans and groans two steps behind us. While Leo takes a call, I'm drawn in by some delicious-smelling candles. The gentleman in the store explains how he makes them.

"Would you like to make one?" he offers.

"I'd love to, thank you."

He shows me the differently shaped moulds, the coloured dyes, and the selection of scented oils he uses to make them smell so good. We get to work, and I'm having a lovely time mixing the scents; for the first time since I've been here, I feel as though I am enjoying myself on holiday.

"A perfect choice. A beautiful candle for a beautiful lady." The gentleman kisses my hand but then abruptly drops it, staring behind me. Leo glares intensely at us from the doorway.

"Leo, come in. Come and smell this; it is absolutely gorgeous. This lovely gentleman here has just shown me how to make my own candle; look how pretty it is." I link Leo's arm with mine and pull his stiff body into the shop. The candle I'm wafting under his nose does nothing for his cold, wide-eyed expression.

"See, doesn't it smell wonderful?" I gush.

"If you say so. We need to get going." He

replies impatiently.

Chapter 8

Katie

The gentleman bags up my candle along with a few other bits I like. Leo insists on paying. We make our way along the street; Leo steers me up a little alley and into a magnificent jewellers'. The whole shop twinkles with diamonds and precious stones in glass cabinets.

"Apparently, my wife-to-be needs a ring."

I follow Leo around the shop as the assistant explains the different areas.

"Over here, you find our solitaire rings, and here are our three stones. Do you have anything specific in mind?"

"Oh, I don't know—maybe something black to match his heart."

The assistant does a half giggle, not knowing whether or not to laugh.

"I'll leave you both to it," she says, sensing the awkwardness.

I have dreamt of this moment since I was a

little girl. But not like this.

Taking a look around, I imagine if this was a real engagement. Which ring would I choose? It has to be a solitaire. Either a square or a round diamond. Platinum, definitely. Wow, there are some stunning rings.

The assistant pulls me from my bubble. "Do you see anything you like?"

I see Leo's dark eyes looking at me with impatience.

"Yes, ummm, this one." I point to a gold ring with three large diamonds. It's pretty, but it's not me.

"Lovely choice." The assistant hands me the ring to try on.

It's huge; it doesn't fit at all.

"No!"

Both the assistant and I jump at Leo's outburst.

"We can have it resized; it won't take long," she says apologetically.

"Not that one; this one here." Leo bangs on the glass cabinet with his finger. "We will take this one."

The assistant places the ring Leo has chosen on my finger, and it fits perfectly. It's also a platinum band with a large round solitaire. I love it.

It's exactly the one I would choose. I don't want it.

"I don't like it."

"Yes, you do." Leo hands his card to the assistant before I can refuse further.

"I told you that you like it," Leo says with a smirk when he catches me admiring it on the journey back.

"Yes, I do like it. I love it, in fact. It's exactly the one I would have chosen. That's why I don't want it."

"I don't understand. Why do you not want it?"

"Because we aren't really engaged. Not properly. I wanted this ring to be given to me by someone who loves me, whom I love. For them to get down on one knee and tell me how much they love me, for them to *ask* me to be their wife. Not force me into it, give me a list of rules, and threaten me with goodness knows what if I don't comply. That's why I don't want it."

For a change, it's not anger on Leo's face. It's confusion mixed with something else.

Leo

Ungrateful. That's what she is. From now on, I will treat this arrangement as I do all my deals. I am in charge. She gets nothing else.

"I will be out for the rest of the day and night. You will stay here. Behave. I have left Van in charge of you. He isn't as friendly as Marco."

I close the bedroom door on her unamused face.

The SUV slowly rolls around the back of the dock. It's dark and quiet. Not for long.

"Everyone is in position, boss. The light in the distance is the cargo arriving."

The moonlight shining on the sea bounces sporadically as the boat approaches.

"On my order." I instruct.

The boat docks. I watch the unsuspecting men unload my delivery, albeit 15 percent less than expected. I let my fury build my adrenaline. Marco watches me through the rearview mirror, waiting for the signal.

"Now!"

The crew shouts, firing their guns into the darkness in panic. They stop once they realise who they are surrounded by.

"Kenny," I say to the member of the crew in charge of the transportation of my delivery.

"Boss, you gave us a bit of a fright there. What's going on?" he replies, trying not to sound worried.

"That is a good question, Kenny. You tell me what has been going on tonight." I command.

The other three crew members look from one another and back to Kenny, terror growing in their eyes.

"Everything to plan, boss."

Boom. The gunfire echoes through the night. The lifeless body hits the deck, increasing the panic in the remaining crew members' eyes.

"Wrong answer, Kenny!"

Boom.

Another body hitting the deck causes Kenny's last remaining crew member to piss himself.

Boom.

"I hate the smell of guilt." I sniff up and spit at Kenny's feet.

Three bodies lie lifeless, blood turning the wooden deck a deep shade of red. I don't need to ask for this mess to be cleaned. By the morning, the deck will be cleaner than it was when we arrived.

"Wrap up Kenny's leg; I don't want him bleeding all over the car or dying before we have a chance to speak."

"But boss, Kenny is not bleeding," Marco replies questioningly.

Boom.

"He is now."

Marco puts a screaming Kenny in the boot of car and drives us to my house. He pulls into the underground garage.

I let the shutter door close before I exit the car. Marco drags Kenny out effortlessly and ties him to a chair.

Marco puts on his bloodstained butcher's apron.

"Just kill me, Guerra." Kenny's voice is weak. He's clearly affected by the loss of blood.

"Now, what would be the fun of that? Marco likes to amuse himself I can't deprive him of that."

Marco examines the tools presented neatly on a table in front of Kenny. Settling into my chair, I light a cigar. Kenny coughs as I blow smoke in his direction.

"Now, Kenny, we all know why we are here. We can do this the painful way or the even more painful way. Which is it going to be?"

Macro approaches Kenny with his tool of choice. His favourite one to begin with—pruning shears. He grabs Kenny's hand, placing his finger between the blades.

"So, what have you got to tell me? Who did you meet? Give me a name!"

"I don't know their name, I swear!"

Crunch. The first finger drops to the floor.

Screams of terror ripple through the soundproof underground garage. A strange uneasiness twinges in my chest. Something is not right. I look around the room at my men, who all have confused looks on their faces.

And then I see her. Katherine exits a cupboard and runs as if her life depends on it up the stairs. She slips halfway, banging her kneecap on the concrete step. I immediately go to help her.

"Don't you touch me!" The disgust is clear in her tone.

"Finish this, Marco." I demand over my shoulder.

I follow Katherine up the stairs. She runs away from me, escaping to our bedroom and locking the door behind her. I could break it down, but I don't, deciding to let her cool off first. I need a drink.

Chapter 9

Katie

Gasping for breath while fighting the urge to throw up, I frantically search for my phone. Got it. I ring Damien, praying he will answer.

"Katie?"

Oh, thank goodness.

"Damien. You need to get me out of here," I whisper while checking the door is still locked.

"I'm working on it."

"No, Damien, you don't understand. I have just seen him cut a man's finger off; well, not him exactly. But it was done at his command."

Ignoring my outburst, Damien continues. "At the moment, we can't find a get-out clause. But if you can get back to England, I can protect you. While you are in Italy, my hands are tied."

"Okay, I can do that. I'll just get my passport and get a flight straight home."

"Katie, Guerra will not let you just walk out

of there and come home. Especially after you have seen what you have tonight."

I can't breathe. I am having a panic attack.

"Katie, listen to me. Everything will be okay. You need to get him to trust you. If you can get yourself to the airport and on a plane to anywhere in the world other than Italy, I can take it from there. While you are on his turf, I'm helpless."

Tears roll from my eyes. I'm shaking, huddled in the corner of the room.

"If I thought he would hurt you, I would have a team there immediately, Katie. But I cannot do that knowing I would lose the lives of my men. Not when I know he won't hurt you."

"How do you know he won't hurt me?"

"Because he chose you."

"I don't understand," I whisper.

"Get him to trust you, Katie. I will ring you tomorrow and see how you're doing. Get some rest."

Remembering the sound of the shears cutting through bone makes me heave. The image of the finger hitting the floor has me hugging the toilet bowl, bringing up everything I can. I cry my heart out, sobbing until my tears dry up. When I return to the bedroom, Leo is sitting on the end of the bed.

I can't look at him. He turns my stomach.

"He was a bad man, Katherine."

"And what are you, Leo?"

I get into bed and turn off the light, hoping he will leave.

"He stole from me. As a result, women and children died. I might not be a good man. But there are far worse."

"Who are you, Leo?"

His tone becomes more aggressive. "You don't understand."

"Try me?"

He is still for a few moments, and I think he is about to open up. But no. He rises and marches to the door.

"Do not ever go down there again. Do you understand me?"

"Yes, boss," I mutter, pulling the covers over my head as he slams the door behind him.

He need not worry. I will not be going down there ever again. Well, they say curiosity killed the cat. That will teach me to be so nosey. It hadn't taken me long to figure out the last number of the bookcase passcode. 2001. The year Leo and I met. Coincidence? Maybe. The guy Leo had left to watch me was as gullible as he was wide. Van was huge. When I said I was going to bed, he believed me and went to work through the contents of the kitchen fridge.

The bookcase led me down stone stairs to a tiled room that smelled of bleach mixed with something putrid. A shutter door filled one side, while tools were neatly lined up on the other three walls, with some set out on a table as if it was a work area—a garage of some sort, I imagined. When the shutter doors started to open, I hid in a cupboard and watched through a crack in the door. Leo looked evil. Devil-like as his cigar smoke circled around him. I couldn't believe my eyes. I couldn't breathe. I heaved at the sight, needing to escape. I doubt I will ever get the image of a finger hitting the floor, blood spurting in all directions, out of my mind.

Having not slept a wink, I put on my sunglasses and throw my beach bag over my shoulder, hoping I can go to the beach. I need to get out of this house and get some fresh air.

"Where do you think you are going?" Leo's voice booms through the hallway.

"The beach."

"I do not think so."

"Are you worried I am going to run off and leave you? I won't get very far, seeing as you have taken my passport!" I know this because I spent all night tearing up the bedroom, looking for it. It had been in the zip pocket of my suitcase, which is now empty.

I continue heading for the front door just as Marco stands and blocks my way.

"Let her go," Leo instructs.

Marco reluctantly moves to the side and opens the door for me.

"Thank you, just Marco. You are such a gentleman." I give him a smile as I escape the madhouse.

The further away from the house I get, the better I feel. I know Leo will have his men watching me, but I just need some air. The sun warming my skin releases the tension in my shoulders. A light breeze fills my lungs with oxygen, and I feel some of my anxiety leave as I breathe out.

A stone-cobbled path leads down steps to the seafront. I'm greeted by white sand and blue sea when I reach the bottom. The sea air makes me smile. It's a quiet beach with a few locals sitting under their own umbrellas. I find a nice spot and set my blanket and towel down. Sitting there, people-watching and taking in the country's beauty, it is hard to believe the horrendous cruelty I witnessed last night.

There's a lady about my age playing with her

son in the sea. They have a dog with them, too, who obviously doesn't like the water, so she just stands there barking at them, running forwards and backwards as the waves go in and out. They look English, but I would presume they live here, since they have a dog. Feeling relaxed, I lie back, enjoying the burn of the sun's rays on my skin. The music from my earphones, mixed with the lack of sleep, soon has me dozing.

A spray of cold water on my hot skin wakes me instantly from my dreams. "Aahh!" I sit up in shock.

Chapter 10

Katie

"MACY!" The lady I was watching earlier with her son comes running over, grabbing the wet, white fluffy dog at my side.

"I'm so sorry. NO, NO, NO!"

Another sprinkle of cold water covers me as Macy shakes her fur at the side of me.

"It's fine, honestly. I needed to cool off."

My skin is looking rather red. I should have put sun cream on before falling asleep; the dog has probably saved me from serious burns.

"You're English?" The lady asks.

"Born and bred."

"Me too. My name is Emmaline; this is Alfie," she replies, introducing her blond blue-eyed boy.

"I'm Katherine, but everyone calls me Katie." Well, almost everyone.

"Katie, please join us for lunch. It's only a picnic, but we have plenty to go around,"

Emmaline offers.

"Oh, thank you, but I wouldn't like to impose; I will just eat when I get back."

"Please, it's the least we can do, since Macy soaked you." Emmaline is a beautiful, friendly soul; I instantly like her. She has big, brown, friendly eyes that make me feel at ease.

For the next hour, we eat meats, breads, and fruit, drinking fresh juices while listening to Alfie tell us jokes.

"Hey, Mum, did you hear about the fight down at the fishing dock?

"No, I didn't hear about that, Alfie."

"Yeah, a fish got battered!" Alfie rolls around in laughter at his own joke.

Emmaline's body language starts to change. I notice she keeps looking over my shoulder. Following her line of sight, I see a man sitting on a rock facing this way. He is wearing sunglasses, a shirt, and trousers. Not dressed for a day at the beach at all. I recognise him as one of Leo's men I have seen at the house.

"We better get going, Alfie."

Emmaline starts to pack up, so I give her a hand.

"We come to the beach most mornings; maybe we will see you again, Katie?" Emmaline seems genuinely hopeful.

"I'd like that." I admit.

When I get back to the house, Marco tells me that Leo is waiting for me in his office. He's sat at his desk, a cloud of cigar smoke surrounding his head and a glass of what looks like whiskey in his hand.

"You have decided to return?" He doesn't look at me, just raises his drink and swills it around. "Sit." He nods to a leather armchair facing his desk.

"Let me explain something to you, Katherine. I am under an obligation to get married. You made me a promise and are therefore obligated to fulfil that promise. As you have witnessed, people lose limbs when they do not do as I have asked. I suggest you behave yourself."

A phone rings on his desk. Leo smirks when he sees the caller ID. He answers immediately.

"Damien King. I have been expecting your call." Leo glares at me whilst he listens, then he shouts, "Enough!" Leo throws his glass across the room. "Do not start a war you will not win, Mr. King. We may be distant relatives, but Katherine owes me a debt, and I am going to collect it!"

He ends the call and focusses on me.

"I have been lenient with you, but I have had

enough of your games. From now on, you will do as I say when I say it. You will not leave this house without me. You will eat all your meals with me. You will be at my side whenever I wish it."

"You can't do this, Leo; I am a person. You can't keep me on a leash like an animal."

"A leash? What a wonderful idea."

"You're a sick man, Leo. You need help!"

"Marco! Take her to our room."

Marco's large hands grip my arms. He lifts me off the ground and carries me from the room. When we are out of earshot, I try to reason with Marco.

"Marco, please. I know you don't like me; you think Leo marrying me is just as crazy as I do, right? There must be something you can do. Please?"

Not saying a word, he continues escorting me to the bedroom. Just as the door closes, I hear Marco speak the softest I have ever heard him.

"There's nothing I can do. He will never let you go."

Chapter 11

Katie

"Ahh.... Ouch.... Oooh." My skin burns as I get into the warm bath water.

Really wishing I had put sun cream on today, I quickly wash and get out of the water, unable to stand the pain. The sight in the mirror is hilarious. If I wasn't so drained, I would laugh. My face is blotchy and puffy; my body is bright red. Blisters have already formed on my back. The cold after-sun lotion on my skin makes me scream.

Crash.

The bathroom door bursts opens. Leo enters with his gun drawn, searching the bathroom.

"I heard screaming." he states.

"That was just me putting on lotion."

"Lotion? Why does putting on lotion make you scream?" Leo's eyes roam my naked body.

I grab a hand towel to cover myself. Anger builds on his face; he turns me around to look at my back. I flinch at his touch.

"Who did this to you?!" His voice is almost a growl.

"Nobody 'did' it to me. I forgot to put on sun cream, so I got a little burnt."

"This is more than a little burnt. Wait here." He disappears out of the bathroom but is back within seconds, holding a little brown bottle.

"Turn around." He instructs impatiently.

I do as he says and turn to face the mirror; Leo stands behind me, studying my back. He rolls up his sleeves, then pours the bottle's contents into his hands. He gently places them on my back, his eyes darting straight to the mirror to see my reaction. I nod for him to continue. Carefully, Leo spreads the lotion over my skin. He's so gentle. Goosebumps spread over my body, my tiny hairs standing to attention. The gesture doesn't fit, coming from the dangerous man behind me.

He has me mesmerised, watching his movements. I notice myself blush as his furrowed brow scans my body. Leo must notice, too, as a smirk crosses his chiselled face. I shouldn't feel this relaxed in the hands of the devil. My body is betraying common sense.

"Why are you doing this, Leo?"

Holding my eyes in the mirror, his mouth brushes my ear. "Kat-er-een. This body belongs to me. I look after my belongings. I do not like my things getting spoilt. In the future, you will look after yourself. Do you understand me?"

"Yes" is all I can manage. His hands leave my body, and he disappears from the bathroom, leaving me breathless.

When I enter the bedroom, he's sat in a chair, reading something on his phone. Wrapped in my robe, I get some pjs out of my case.

"You may as well unpack properly; you're not going anywhere."

"Get out!" I scream.

Leo laughs at my outburst. How can he make me so relaxed one minute and the next so infuriated?

He strides over to stand right in front of me, he cups my face. His touch instantly sends me back to being a teenager. For a moment my feelings come flooding back. But it doesn't last long. His next words bring me back to reality.

"I am going nowhere, Katherine. And neither are you."

"Don't touch me!" I bat away his hands.

Smirking, he releases me.

"You don't want me to touch you? That's not the impression I got five minutes ago. Five minutes ago, your skin tingled and pimpled at my touch; it flushed under my gaze."

"Don't flatter yourself. My skin crawled at your touch and flushed through fright. I was just too scared to tell you to stop."

His eyes hold mine for a moment. I think I see hurt, or is it anger? The moment passes, and he leaves the room, slamming the door and locking it behind him.

I curl up in bed and try to sleep. This is a nightmare.

Waking up to the sound of a message alert on my phone, I realise I've slept through the full night. It must be all the sun I got yesterday. I pick up my phone and read the message.

Leo: Breakfast in the dining room, 10 minutes.

I throw my phone across the bed in frustration.

∞ ∞ ∞

"You're late," Leo states when I arrive twenty minutes later, not looking up from his breakfast.

I don't bother to reply. I took my time showering and getting ready, not caring about pleasing him. Alga serves me my breakfast choice from the spread she has laid out on the table.

Answering Alga is the only time I speak. I can feel Leo glaring into the side of my head, but I don't look at him.

Marco enters the room.

"I need a word."

Leo nods for him to go ahead. But Marco stares at me.

"Lei non puo capirti." *She cannot understand you.* Leo waves for him to continue.

Huh, that's what they think.

Marco reluctantly informs Leo that a large cargo they had due to be delivered today has not made it. The cargo ship has been found in the middle of the ocean, empty with all the crew members dead. I can see Leo is trying to keep calm in my presence, so I leave the room while Leo blames Marco for not preventing the disaster and not having found the culprit already.

Out on the patio, the morning sun is already warm on my skin. The lotion Leo used has really helped my burns. The garden and pool look beautiful; it's a real paradise out here. If only I could enjoy it. If only I wasn't being forced to live with a dangerous criminal. Why couldn't he be the kind, caring, funny boy I first met? I miss home, my friends. I miss work; I miss my life.

Leo joins me, taking a seat at my side. He lights a cigar, something I have noticed he does when he is stressed.

I make conversation. "Bad news?"

"You could say that."

We sit in silence while I finish my coffee and he finishes his smoke.

"Tonight we are attending an opera. I have a designer arriving at 11:00; you will choose an outfit. She will alter it where needed and have it ready in time."

I've always wanted to go to the opera, but I don't let him know this.

I'm waiting in the front room when the designer arrives, pulling a long rail of dresses. Two other girls follow behind her, keeping their heads down, looking very uncomfortable. Marco closes the door behind them, then stands in front of the door with his arms folded.

The designer shows me the dresses, but I can tell she and the girls are very on edge with Marco in the room.

"Marco, please leave." I say with as much confidence as I can.

Marco glares at me.

"Would you mind giving me some privacy?"

"My orders are to guard the door. Guard the door, I will."

"Well, how about you guard the other side

of the door? I'm sure Leo wouldn't be happy if he heard you had been watching his fiancée undress and looking at her naked breasts?"

"I won't—"

I cut him off before he finishes that sentence by quickly removing my vest top, revealing my breasts; he can't help but let his eyes land on them.

Quickly remembering himself, he covers his eyes. Fumbling around with his eyes still closed, he opens the door.

"I'll be right on the other side!" He groans.

The girls visibly relax as soon as the door closes.

"These are the dresses I have selected as per Mr. Guerra's suggestions. Choose your favourite, and I will ensure it fits you perfectly." The designer explains while taking each dress from the rail.

All the dresses are lovely but very conservative and not at all me. If Leo wants to marry me, then he is going to marry the real me whether he likes it or not. There's only one dress that catches my eye. It's red silk. I love bright, bold colours. I usually have my hair a bright colour, pink was my last, but it has faded out to my natural blonde now. Red will be the perfect statement for me.

"I want this one, but I'd like a few changes." I say holding it against my body.

"Changes?"

"Yes. I love the halter neck, but I would like the neckline to plunge about three inches lower."

"Okay?" The designer takes out a pen and paper.

"And the back—I'd like that to be much lower too. Just above my bottom will be perfect, and a split in one side of the skirt area up to my hip."

She narrows her eyes at me.

"Miss, Mr. Guerra gave me strict instructions on the type of dress I was to bring here today. I'm not sure he would be happy with these types of alterations."

"With all due respect, I am Mr. Guerra's fiancée. Soon to be Mrs. Guerra. I'm sure my husband-to-be only wants me to be happy, do you not agree?"

The designer nods, clearly confused.

"So, can you do it or not?"

She looks to her assistants, who shrug. I feel a little bad for being so pushy, but I know I wouldn't get what I want otherwise.

"Okay, I can do it." She agrees.

"Fabulous." I smile.

After having my measurements taken, the dress cut and pinned into its new style, shoes and accessories chosen, I hit the gym feeling pretty pleased with myself.

Chapter 12

Katie

"Katherine!" Leo bellows through the house, his voice penetrating the closed bedroom door.

I take one last look at myself in the mirror as well as a deep breath. I feel sick with nerves; maybe this dress wasn't such a good idea after all.

My makeup makes my eyes pop, and my skin looks flawless. My hair is pinned up in loose curls to reveal the open back and plunging neckline. The designer has done an amazing job. The silk dress fits perfectly. Thanks to Leo's lotion, my burnt skin now looks sun-kissed. I look pretty good.

I pick up my clutch bag, put my chin up, and confidently walk to the front door, where Leo waits for me. I purposely made us late, putting on my dress at the last minute so Leo wouldn't have a chance to make me change. I walk past a few of Leo's men, who take second looks; I can feel their eyes on me as I walk. My high-heeled sandals click on the marble floor, notifying Leo and Marco of my arrival.

"Finally," Leo states with a half glance before he turns again to look at me, wide-eyed.

Marco is standing at his side. He takes me in and then looks at Leo. A small smirk appears on Marco's face. A smirk. It is the first time I have seen any emotion on that sour man's face. Leo looks me up and down as I walk, noticing my left leg reveal itself with each step. His eyes on my body make me flush. He looks so handsome wearing a black fitted suit, crisp white shirt, and black bow tie. But his face is thunder.

"Ready to go?" I smile.

"Kat-er-een! This is not the type of dress I had in mind."

"Oh really? I love it." I do a little twirl, and as I do, I see we have an audience behind us.

"What is everyone looking at?! Get out!" Leo spins me around, his body obscuring their view. "You need to get changed," he grumbles at me.

"We have no time for that; she looks fine. Let's go," Marco says as he walks towards our waiting car.

I follow him quickly before Leo marches me back to our room. I get in the car, leaving the door open for him to slide in beside me. For a minute, I think he isn't going to come, but eventually, he lets out a big sigh and climbs in.

It takes about fifteen minutes to get to the

theatre; Leo doesn't say a word to me the whole way. The car pulls up to a red carpet at the front entrance. He holds his hand out to help me from the car. I reluctantly place my small hand in his large palm. A tingling sensation shocks me as our skin touches, making me jump, I try to pull my hand away, but he holds on to it tightly.

His wide eyes meet mine, then he pulls me towards him. "That split in your dress is far too high," he whispers into my ear.

"Oh really? And I forgot to put underwear on too. Whoops!"

My statement stuns him into letting go of my hand. I quickly make my way up the steps before he can catch me. I hear him roar and slam the car door. Marco walks up beside me and holds me back to wait for Leo.

"You are a bad girl, Kat-er-een. You do not leave my side all night, do you hear me?" Leo growls into my ear.

"Yes." I smile, greeting the doormen and other guests as we enter.

We are shown into a large reception room. Waiters offer champagne and canapes on silver trays. All eyes are on us while we make our way through the room.

"What would you like to drink, Katherine?" Leo lightly touches the bare skin on my back as he gently directs me toward the bar.

I smile.

"Why are you smiling?"

"It's nice to be asked what I would like for a change. A gin and tonic would be lovely, thank you."

We stand at the bar and sip our drinks. A couple of gentlemen come over and speak to Leo and Marco in Italian—mostly business.

One man receives a death threat when he comments on my bottom.

With a smile on his face, Leo whispers to the man, still unaware I speak Italian. "If you look at my fiancée in that way again, I will rip out your eyes and feed them to the birds. Now get out before I let Marco take you out."

He then friendly slaps him on the shoulder and tells him to have a good night. The man was very creepy, so I am glad he sent him on his way.

"Signore e signori, vi prego di prendere posto. Juan Diego Florez sta per iniziare."

Ladies and gentlemen, please, will you take your seats. Juan Diego Florez is about to begin.

We are seated in a private box with a fantastic stage view. I notice people take a second glance as we claim our seats. Some people in the tiers below us seem to leave the theatre after recognising Leo.

The lights dim in readiness for the show to begin.

Leo leans in and whispers in my ear. "You look beautiful."

The compliment surprises me. I feel myself blush. I don't look at him, but I can feel his eyes on me. I don't respond with words, but I'm sure he can see the effect he has on me. Why does my body continue to rebel against my common sense?

I'm soon fully immersed in the opera; the emotions I'm experiencing are really unexpected. It's so powerful. I'm crying at the tragedy, laughing at the comedy, and gasping at the surprises. The final part of one of the songs has everyone on their feet; it's incredible how the audience is connecting to the music. It gets louder, and I can feel the rhythm vibrating through my body.

Bang! Bang!

Painful pressure in my chest brings me out of the emotional trance. Agony shoots through my head. I hear screams. My ears ring with noise, but it is no longer the beautiful music; it's the sound of panic and pain—high-pitched, frenzied cries.

Bang! Bang!

Terror fills me.

I can't see anything. I am struggling to get my breath; it's hard to expand my lungs. I'm trapped.

"Stay down until I say move."

Eventually I realise Leo's body covers mine, he is the pressure I feel, the reason I can't fully expand my ribcage to breathe. My head is pressed against the floor. Why is he doing this to me? I'm confused. I have no idea what is going on. A few more minutes pass, and my head feels light with the lack of oxygen. I want to scream for help, to thrash out, but the weight is too much for my strength.

Just before losing consciousness, I'm lifted into the air. My body is held close to a chest, my face pressed into a neck—Leo's neck. His smell fills my senses. I grab hold of his suit as he runs downstairs and out into the now cool night air. A car beeps as it is unlocked, the hold on me loosens, and I'm placed gently but quickly into the passenger seat. Leo fastens my seat belt before quickly rounding the car, jumping into the driver's seat, and starting the car in record time. We speed out of the car park and join a busy road.

"Are you hurt?!"

His abrupt question makes me jump. I open my mouth, but nothing comes out. There was pain, but I'm mostly just sore now. I look down at myself; I look okay; there's no blood. I ache, but that's about it.

"Katherine! Look at me! You're okay. You are

safe now."

My body shakes uncontrollably. All I can do is stare out of the window. The street and car lights we pass form coloured streams in front of my eyes. I try to process what has happened. The night's events are jumbled in my memory; I struggle to make sense of it.

Leo opens my door. We've arrived back at the house. He lifts me out of the car and carries me in.

We go into the living room. He sits down on the sofa with me on his lap. His fingers gently move across my face, pushing my hair out of my eyes.

"You are in shock. I promise you are safe now."

Alga comes in, pushing a trolley of refreshments.

"Here, drink this."

I take a sip of the sweet tea and settle back down on his lap.

"Come, let's get you more comfortable."

Carrying me again, he walks into the bedroom, then sets me down gently by the bed. He takes my face in his hands; his eyes are wide. I brace myself for what he is about to say.

A crash echoes through the house.

"Marco is back." Leo drops his hands, and

his hard expression returns. "Get changed. Stay in here. I will be back soon." He leaves the room.

I shower, get my pjs on, and snuggle my teddy in bed. The TV takes my mind off the night events until I hear Marco and Leo's raised voices. I get up and press my ear to the door, straining to make out what they are saying.

They are speaking in Italian. Marco is furious. He is accusing Leo of losing his mind. That I am a distraction. It seems it was a couple of gang members trying to rise in the hierarchy, thinking they'd get a shot at the Don and gain themselves some street cred—only, both men received a bullet between their eyes from Marco. Marco is furious that Leo did not retaliate, that he threw himself over me, which apparently was a detrimental decision. After a few more minutes of crossed words, I hear Marco leave.

When I'm feeling more settled after watching some crazy Italian TV show, I settle down to sleep. Leo hasn't returned, and I doubt he will now, after his argument with Marco. Despite the night's traumatic event, I manage to fall into a blissful sleep—until I am woken by the sound of heart-harrowing moans of distress.

Chapter 13

Katie

Painful cries sound in my ears. I'm half asleep, so it takes me a while to realise I'm not dreaming. The noise is coming from a man. A man in this room. At first, the noises sounded far away, but they're not. They're muffled slightly, but close. My bed bounces and rocks. There is someone next to me, thrashing about. Apprehensive about who it may be, I turn slowly to see who is in the bed beside me. I see a tanned, toned bare back. It glistens with sweat beneath the moonlight with each move it makes. It's stretching and clenching. The smell of cigars and alcohol mixed with Leo fills my nose.

"Leo?" I touch his shoulder gently.

He turns towards me. Still asleep, his face is full of pain. "No!" He wimpers.

His cry has me holding his head, whispering calming words, and stroking his hair. The thrashing and moans begin to calm.

"Hey, it's okay, it's me, Katherine."

Leo's eyes open, they connect with mine, and I see him. I see the old Leo. All the barriers are down, and the beautiful soul I first met is back. Cuddling into me, he lays his head on my chest as I continue running my fingers through his hair.

"What were you dreaming about?" I don't expect him to answer.

"My brother."

I remember him having a brother; Leo spoke of him a lot when we wrote to each other. They were very close.

"Alex, isn't it?"

Leo's breathing picks up. He takes in a deep breath and sighs. "I haven't heard his name in years." His voice is pained.

I wrap my arms around him and squeeze, holding him as close to me as I can. I'm unsure of what to say, but I know he needs this. "Do you remember when we used to lie like this, falling asleep under the stars?"

"Come se fosse ieri." *Like it was yesterday.*

Leo's breathing slows, signifying sleep is upon him. It doesn't take long for me to follow.

When I wake, Leo is gone, but I find him sitting at the dining table.

"Good morning, Katherine. Did you sleep

well?"

"Very well, thank you."

Alga is finishing up laying out breakfast on the table. She smiles at me like she knows something I don't.

I feel hungry this morning, so I go for a full English breakfast. While devouring the delicious food, I catch Leo staring at me from the corner of my eye.

"What are you looking at?" I question while biting into a piece of toast.

"Are you enjoying that?"

"Yes, why?"

"You know you make a humming noise when you eat?"

"I do not!" I protest.

"You do—like this: *HUMMMM*." Leo mimics me.

"No, I don't."

I laugh and throw the slice of toast I'm holding at him. I panic for a second, remembering who he is, but he soon picks up the piece, laughing. He takes a bite and throws it back. We end up having a mini food fight, with Leo pulling me onto his lap and rubbing jam on my nose.

That's the moment when Marco walks in.

"What the fuck is going on here!" He says.

"I'll leave you guys to it." I say, standing from Leo's lap.

"No! You will stay here and finish your breakfast."

Okay, the old Leo has once again left the building.

I sit in silence, eating as quickly as I can so I can get out of there. Marco and Leo are arguing in Italian. Marco says Leo needs to be making his presence known at his warehouses and delivery points. He needs to show whoever is intercepting his deliveries that he is the one in charge; the people need to know that the Guerras are still in control. Leo refuses and has a go at Marco for trying to tell him what to do. Once my plate is clear, I take it into the kitchen and have a coffee with Alga and Sergio.

"You're good for him, you know." Alga rubs my arm as she passes me the sweetener.

"I don't think Marco thinks so. Plus, Leo is no good for me."

"He's a good man under all that darkness. I think you're the one to show him the light."

I'm not sure about Alga's statement, but I'm starting to hope my Leo is still in there somewhere.

Leo joins us in the kitchen.

"What are your plans for today, Katherine?" Leo asks.

"Plans? I didn't think I was allowed to make plans. I'm not supposed to leave the house without you, remember?"

"Where would you like to go today?" He puts his hand on my shoulder.

"Home?"

Leo grimaces at my comment, so I change my answer, not wanting to put him in a bad mood. "The beach, then. I found this lovely little spot the other day."

"The beach it is. Alga, we are going to the beach."

Leo disappears, and Alga shouts after him, "Give me ten minutes."

Alga and Sergio rush about the kitchen; I leave them to it.

Once I'm ready to go, I find Alga at the door with a cooler bag, no doubt full of refreshments and tasty treats.

"Thank you, Alga."

I hear Leo approach; I'm taken back by the sight of him. He's wearing swim shorts—yes, *short* swim shorts, displaying his tanned, toned legs sprinkled with dark hair. A white T-shirt moulds over the mounds of his torso.

"Wow." Oops, did I say that out loud?

Leo raises one eyebrow at me. "Wow? Katherine?" There's amusement in his voice.

"You look different, that's all. I've never seen you in short shorts before."

"Short shorts?" Leo smirks. "Well, you didn't expect me to wear a three-piece suit to the beach, did you?"

I think I may be blushing. My cheeks feel hot.

"Let's get going." I open the front door, needing a distraction from my embarrassment.

Leo's large hand moves swiftly over my shoulder and slams it shut before I have a chance to get out.

"Not so fast."

He spins me round and holds me with my back against the door, his front against mine.

"Are you going to be a good girl today, Katherine?"

A gasp leaves my throat as he presses his hard body against mine even more. He tucks hair behind my ear and follows the path of his fingers with his mouth, his lips brushing my ear lobe.

"Have you packed your sun cream?"

That is not what I suspected him to say.

"Yes."

"Good. Let's go, then."

He moves me to the side and opens the door, leaving me standing there, watching him walk down the drive. He is playing with me. Well, two can play this game, Mister. Bring it on.

Once we arrive, Leo chooses a nice alcove in the rocks to relax in. Apparently, it has a good view of the beach, and no one can approach us from behind without us noticing.

While I'm applying my sun cream, Leo snatches the bottle from me.

"Turn around."

I willingly do so, looking forward to feeling his hands on my body again. He begins with my shoulders, his large, strong hands massaging my skin as if needing to touch every nerve, muscle, and bone beneath it. He then moves up to my neck; he squeezes and rubs my nape, which sends tingles down my body. Both hands then grip my neck. Anyone else would panic at this action from such a dangerous man, but my head automatically tips back, a moan escaping as my body melts into his hands. I hope no one is watching, because my face must be pornographic.

"Okay, your turn now." I gesture to the blanket laid out on the sand. Reluctantly, with a smirk and a raised eyebrow, he lies on his front.

Showtime.

I straddle him. Only the thin material of my bikini separates the heat between my legs and the skin on his back.

"Katherine. What are you doing?" The question comes out in a growl.

"I'm putting your cream on. Just lie there and relax."

I start at his shoulders and work down his arms; I put my all into each movement, squeezing my thighs around his legs to hold my balance. I work my way down to the bottom of his back, my fingertips tracing lightly over his scars. One day I will ask him about each and every one of those. I dip my fingers slightly under the waistband of his shorts.

In one swift movement, Leo spins onto his back beneath me on the blanket. His eyes now locked with mine, he holds my hips down, my warmth pressing into his very hard, thick length. "Do not start something you cannot finish, Kat-er-een."

He bucks his hips into me. I gasp. He smirks and flips me over so I'm now the one lying on the blanket with him straddling me. He leans in. His nose touches mine. Our eyes connect. He licks his lips. He grinds ever so slightly. The groan that leaves his body vibrates into mine. My body is melting beneath him.

We stay like this for a moment. Our breathing has picked up. Emotion builds in his eyes. But in a flash, he breaks the connection, and it's gone.

"I'm going for a swim," he declares and then he's up and off, running into the sea, leaving my body begging. I hate him.

While he is cooling off in the sea, I people-watch. A man selling fruit and drinks approaches me.

"You like anything to drink, beautiful lady?"

"Oh no, thank you. I have some drinks." I pat the cooler bag.

"Some fruit?"

"No, thank you."

"How about you give me your phone number?"

"No, sorry—and please, will you leave, because if the guy I'm with sees you talking to me, I fear for your life."

Too late.

I spot Leo striding out of the sea, running a hand through his hair as he heads our way. God, he looks hot with water dripping down his tanned body.

"Oh yeah? Who is the guy you are with?" The beach seller chuckles to himself, puffing out his chest.

I nod in Leo's direction.

All the colour drains from the seller's face when he sees Leo.

"Ooooohhh, shit!" He drops all his boxes and runs for his life.

Leo arrives with a smirk on his face.

"Ahh, you got us some more refreshments. You know, Alga would have packed us plenty; there really wasn't any need for more." He sits down beside me.

"He was harmless; there's really no need to hold any of this against him."

"What do you mean, Kat-er-een?"

"You know, don't hurt him or anything. He didn't do anything wrong."

"He approached and no doubt propositioned the fiancée of Leonardo Guerra. That has a punishment of death."

Chapter 14

Katie

"Oh no, please, Leo, don't—I beg you. Please."

Leo's serious expression turns into a laugh.

"You are very easy to wind up, Kat-er-een. I'm not completely evil, you know. I'm not a good person, either, but I have reasons for what I do. Plus, I think his fear of what might happen to him will be punishment enough."

"What is it, exactly, that you do?"

Leo looks at me, eyebrows furrowed. He's clearly contemplating how much to tell me.

"I am the leader of the Guerra organisation. We rule everything in our territory, from the drug dealers on the streets to the highest-level government officials. We provide protection for those who require it while eradicating problems efficiently."

"So you sell drugs, corrupt the government with blackmail, probably, charge people money for not killing them, and kill anyone that stands in your way?"

Leo is visibly annoyed by my interpretation.

"No, that is not how it works," he huffs.

"Well, explain it to me then."

Leo sighs—though, really, it's more of a growl. He leans back on his hands and looks out to sea.

"The world will never be a perfect place, Katherine. There will always be good, and there will always be evil. Both are needed; there cannot be one without the other. The police and government cannot stop or control all crime, drug dealing, or human trafficking. But we can. We ensure all drugs which are sold are safe and of good quality. I only import the best. We do not sell to children. We keep crime rates at a low because if you steal from the corner shop, you are stealing from me. I despise human trafficking; I do not tolerate it, which is more than I can say for our rivals. Truth be told, this isn't the life I would have chosen for myself. I wasn't born to rule. That was my brother. But when he passed, the duty fell on to me."

Stunned into silence, I open the cooler bag and take out two bottles of water. I hand Leo one and take a drink of mine. I'm unsure what I expected him to say, but it wasn't that. I actually kind of understand, which shocks the hell out of me.

"I have done a lot of bad and cruel things, and I will continue to do so. But I have done these things to bad people so that I can protect the good ones."

Lying down on the blanket, I close my eyes to shield them from the sun. Leo lies beside me, his arm and fingers slightly touching mine. A tingle runs through me.

"I don't expect you to understand or agree, Katherine. But you will need to accept it, and I swear, I will never hurt you; you will forever have my protection." He turns on his side, and I can feel him watching me.

"You know, Leo, I have dreamt about this for so many years. I prayed that one day we would find each other. I've imagined lying on a beach with you again so many times."

"Do not lie to me." He slumps back down onto his back.

I sit up to look at him. "I'm not lying. What do you mean?"

He sits up, staring at me hard. He's guarded again in Guerra mode. "I came looking for you. I saw you with him. You had moved on."

"What, when?"

"I hadn't heard from you for months, years; my letters were sent back. My phone calls went unanswered. As soon as I was able, I flew to

England. I found you. You had changed your name and were living with some guy—Paul?"

"Paul?" I laugh.

"I don't find this funny, Kat-er-een. During the days I wasted my time searching for you, my brother was being hunted down and killed." He stands up and walks away; he's so angry.

"Leo, wait."

He continues to walk away from me.

I run after him. "Please, Leo, let me explain."

"There is nothing to explain. Pack up, we are leaving."

"No!"

"No?!" Leo turns; he looks twice his size, so fierce.

Pushing down the fear filling my body, I stand my ground.

"If I am to be your wife, Leonardo Guerra, you will respect me and listen to me."

He tilts his head to one side but says nothing, so I continue.

"Paul is my dad. And the reason I never answered your calls and letters was because we were evicted from our home. I came home from school one day, and everything I owned had gone. I was left with nothing. Believe me; I fought so hard to get my belongings; the only things I actually cared about were my letters from you. My mum had got herself in a mess with the wrong guy yet again, but that's a story for another time. It was the last straw for my dad, so he took me in. I didn't change my name. My dad has always called me Katie; it's a nickname, like Leo, short for Leonardo?"

He stands tall, staring right through me, obviously processing what I have just said.

"Come on, let's sit back down and have something to eat."

He doesn't move. Just looks at me. I calmly walk towards him and take his hand. He lets me guide him back to the blanket.

We sit together, and I get out the food Alga has made. Leo takes the sandwich I offer him but doesn't eat. Just stares out to sea. Deciding not to push him, I make small talk about the food Alga has made, how much I have enjoyed her cooking, and how lucky he is to have live-in help. Growing up, I lived off super noodles and cheese on toast until I moved in with Dad. When living with my mum, we'd go from one month having hardly any money to the next living in luxury. It all depended on how wealthy Mum's boyfriend at the time was. Most days, I'd make my own meals, so it was whatever we had in and the easiest. My parents were only teenagers when they had me; they did the best they could.

Curiosity fills me. I need to know what happened when he came to find me. I need to know what happened to his brother. Our silence is broken when a wet fluff ball comes and sticks her nose in our picnic.

"Macy! Get back here!" I hear Emmaline shout.

"Oh, hello again, Macy dog," I greet my little friend. She's so cute.

Emmaline and Alfie make their way over to us.

"I'm so sorry—oh, hi, Katie. It's good to see you again."

At this point, Macy is climbing on Leo, trying to lick his face. I worry for a second, but he soon starts stroking her and rubbing her ears.

"Hi, Emmaline, Alfie, it's nice to see you again too. This is Leo." I gesture to Leo, who seems quite taken with their dog.

Emmaline does a double-take, her face flushing. I'm not sure if it's because she knows who Leo is or it's just the fact that he is incredibly hot sitting here in his tiny swim shorts.

Leo's phone rings.

"Excuse me for a few minutes." Leo walks away while he speaks.

"Come join me, guys. We've so much food

here, and I owe you from last time."

Emmaline and Alfie both help me make a small dint in the amount of food we have. With the box full of fruit and refreshments plus the picnic Alga made us, which could feed about ten people, we have far too much.

"Can I go look for some crabs, Mum?"

"Sure, just be careful you don't slip on the rocks. And don't go too far out!" Emmaline shouts after Alfie, who is already making his way along the breakwater.

"Katie, how long have you known Leo for?"

"A long time, actually. Well, we met about fifteen years ago and have met up again recently."

"Ahh, so… you know who Leo is, right?"

I sigh. "Yes, I know."

Bark! Bark!

The sound of barking fills my ears.

"Is that Macy?" I ask.

Macy is in the sea, barking frantically. Macy does not like the water, yet she is running into the waves.

"Oh my god, Alfie!" Emmaline makes a run for the water.

I see Alfie lying half on the rocks and half in the sea.

He isn't moving, apart from a slight sliding movement as he is edged further into the waves.

Out of the corner of my eye, I see a flash of olive skin. It's Leo. He is running along the wall of rocks, each step a fast, precise movement. He reaches Alfie, lifts him with ease, and more slowly and carefully carries him back to the beach. Macy follows barking behind them.

After placing him in his mother's arms, he checks him over. Emmaline cries and falls to her knees. Leo supports them both, settling them in the sand.

Leo calls his name. "Alfie, can you hear me? Alfie?"

Emmaline just holds him. She is clearly in shock and has no idea what to do.

Leo checks his pulse and then checks his head.

Emmaline starts to panic. Her breathing becomes erratic. "We need to get him to a hospital."

"Emmaline, look at me." Leo instructs. She instantly does as he says. Even during such a traumatic event, Leo still commands the power.

"Alfie is going to be fine. He has a small cut with a bump on his head. He's just knocked himself out for a while." As Leo talks, Alfie begins to stir. "My team will be here shortly—ahh here they are now." Leo nods in Marco's direction. He is with a guy I don't recognise carrying a green medical bag.

I back away to give them some room; I feel useless just standing here. There's a crowd starting to gather around.

"The boy will be fine. Thank you for your concern. Please give the family some privacy," the guy with the medical bag says as he moves people out of the way.

The crowd quickly disperses except for one man. Leo glares at him, but he doesn't get the message. He then gets his phone out; surely, he can't be taking a photo.

"Are you deaf? Leave!" The man jumps as Leo snatches his phone from his hand and throws it into the sea.

After a few minutes, Alfie is fully awake, thank goodness. Leo arranges for Marco and the medic to take them home and for the medic to stay until Alfie is out of danger. I pack up their things from the beach and get Macy's lead on. We follow Marco, who is carrying Alfie, and the medic, who talks to Emmaline as they walk up the beach and then gets them settled in the SUV. I'm amazed at Leo's prompt organisation.

"You saved the boy's life, Leo." Grabbing his arm, I give it a little squeeze. "How did you get Marco and that medic here so quickly?"

"I was on the phone with Marco when I heard Macy barking. We have a medic available at all times in case of emergencies. I did what needed to be done."

Not sure why I'm surprised this situation hasn't fazed him, I pack up our things, trying to hide my anxiety.

"How brilliant is their Macy dog. If she hadn't alerted everyone, goodness knows what would have happened." I shudder at the thought. "I'd love a dog like Macy. I've always wanted a dog."

"A Guerra will have what they desire. I will instruct Marco to bring the dog back with him. She shall be yours."

"What?! No, you can't do that!"

"Believe me, Katherine, I can do whatever I want. A dog is an insignificant price to pay for saving her son's life. I doubt she will argue."

"Don't you dare, Leo! She is as much her baby as Alfie is. Please don't!" I cry until I see him smirking.

"Ahh, dear Katherine. You are so easy to wind up."

"You're a monster!"

"You're right; I am a monster. Let's go."

At home during dinner, we really start to

connect. Leo tells me about his brother, Alex. Alex was the elder of the two brothers. He was a born leader, according to Leo. A strong, loyal man who lived and breathed the Guerra family and all it represented. Alex had met and fallen in love with the Guerras' archenemy's daughter. Unaware of who their families were at first, the couple had a relationship, and they fell deeply in love. When they realised who each other was, it was too late. They were one. Leo's father was not happy at first, but he declared a truce for his son. The Guerra and the Martelé families would rule beside each other but never together.

When Leo was in England looking for me, Martelé murdered his brother. Alex's girlfriend or recent fiancée killed herself later that day, for whatever reason. Leo speaks with such hatred for her. He doesn't tell me specifics, but he obviously blames her for his death.

The layers are slowly peeling away. He's letting me in. I actually forget that this is a man basically holding me hostage, forcing me into an arranged marriage, threatening me with legal action, and worse. He brings me back to reality when he tells me my plans for tomorrow.

"You're having lunch with my mother tomorrow. Then you will get measured for your wedding dress. You will be wearing a dress I select. Past experiences have taught me you can't be trusted where clothing is concerned. I will not have my wife exposing herself."

My knife and fork drop from my hands, making loud clanging sounds as they hit my plate. Not knowing what to say, I stare at him, my mouth presumably half open at his audacity.

"It's bad enough you have had sexual relations with three other men."

What the actual hell? How does he know I have slept with three other men?

"Don't look surprised, Katherine. You know I am a man of many means. Of course I would want to know what my future wife has been up to."

"This is unbelievable." I stand up to leave, but Leo grabs my wrist.

"Where are you going? We haven't finished our dinner."

Tears fill my eyes. I'm so angry and frustrated. I look him in the eye.

"Why are you doing this, Leo?"

He drops my arm, so I return to our room. As I climb into bed, my phone pings with a message.

Damien: We've found a loophole. We just need to get you back to the UK. Working on it. Hang tight. Damien.

Thank goodness. Hopefully, it won't be much longer now, then. I'll keep my head down and my mouth shut. Cuddling my teddy, I fall asleep feeling more optimistic that this nightmare will be over soon.

I don't speak to Leo at breakfast. He didn't come to our room last night, or I didn't notice if he did, anyway. I slept well, and I'm feeling better after the news from Damien. Leo's mother turns up looking very glamorous in a white trouser suit.

"Katherine! I'm so looking forward to today." She brings me into a hug. I reluctantly return the gesture. "We are going to have so much fun!"

"Van will be with you today, Katherine, as Marco and I have some business to attend to. There will also be someone from my mother's team. Enjoy, ladies. Treat yourselves; anything you like is yours." Leo kisses his mum's cheek.

"Ha!" Anything I like, when he's already told me I have no say in my dress. They both look at me quizzically. I don't say another word, just smile. It doesn't matter anyway; this wedding is not happening.

On the ride into town, Leo's mum makes small talk. A nod and a smile is all she gets in return. I now resent the beautiful Italian views which once filled me with excitement and happiness. I've never wanted to see the grey English weather more than I do now.

The bridal shop is very elegant. It's a place you would dream of getting your wedding dress from. Only for me, this is a nightmare.

My measurements are taken, and then the shop assistants rush around, showing us different gowns while we sit and drink champagne. Well, Leo's mother does; she is in her element.

"Which would you like to try on, Katherine?"

"None of them." I reply sadly.

"You haven't seen anything you like?"

"Oh, I've seen many I like, but Leo has made it quite clear he will be choosing my dress, so there's no point."

The shop assistant looks at me sympathetically.

"Give us some time to discuss, please." Mrs. Guerra ushers them away, then asks, "What is the matter, Katherine?"

"Are you seriously asking me that question?"

Mrs. Guerra sits up a little straighter, obviously annoyed with my tone.

Feeling a little guilty for taking it out on her, but more so, scared of insulting such a powerful woman, I decide to apologise. "I'm sorry. I'm just finding this all very overwhelming."

She stands up and grabs my bag. "Let's go for lunch."

The restaurant Mrs. Guerra takes us to is

only a couple of doors down from the dress shop. All the staff fuss around us the minute we walk through the door. A waiter pours Mrs. Guerra some wine and then moves to do the same for me.

"Oh, not for me, thank you." I put my hand over my glass.

Mrs. Guerra bats it away. "Yes, you will. You need to relax."

Okay, then. The waiter fills my glass.

A range of Italian dishes are brought to our table. We both eat in silence until Mrs. Guerra begins to talk.

"Leo was always a mummy's boy. So kind, thoughtful, and caring. As a child, he loved to draw and paint. We spent our days together, crafting and using our imagination. Leo was always the complete opposite of his brother Alex. Alex was always playing some sort of sport. He was forever coming home covered in cuts and bruises after scrapping with his friends. Alex had an air about him that made people stop and pay attention. He bloomed at a young age. By thirteen, he had started shaving and his voice was so deep, you would think he was a fully grown adult. Other boys looked up to him, Leo especially." Mrs. Guerra is emotional when she speaks. After taking a large sip of her wine she continues.

"The day Alex died, so did Leo. He knew he needed to step up. Since that day, he has been put through the most gruelling training to turn him into the man he is today. It breaks my heart that I have lost both of my boys. It pains me that my boy can no longer be his true self. My husband is dying. He is very weak. The Guerra family needs a strong leader, which is now Leo. He needs a strong, loyal wife by his side. That is you. I will teach you everything you need to know about being a Guerra woman."

"But Leo doesn't love me. I don't love him. Why me? Why do I have to be the Guerra woman?"

"Love is a weakness. He doesn't need love. He needs a tough, strong-willed woman. Someone for the people to look up to and respect."

"But what if I don't want to?"

Mrs. Guerra looks at me and smiles. "Oh, Katherine—you do want to. I see the way you look at my son. You just don't know it yet."

She is so wrong. Cutting up a piece of chicken on my plate to avoid eye contact and the need to reply, I notice the meat is undercooked in the middle, so I push it to one side of my plate.

Mrs. Guerra notices my action and takes a closer look at the chicken.

"Lesson number one. Guerras are to be respected. We are the leaders, and people must be shown that. Send the chicken back."

At a click of her fingers, a waiter appears at

our table.

"I'm sorry, but the chicken isn't quite cooked," I say politely.

Mrs. Guerra rolls her eyes while I continue.

"Could we get a new one or cook this—" I'm cut off midsentence.

"Are you trying to poison us?" Mrs. Guerra snaps, interrupting me.

The waiter apologises profoundly, I can see fear in his eyes; I feel extremely guilty. When he leaves, Mrs. Guerra continues.

"We do not apologise for something we have not done, Katherine. We don't even apologise for something we have done, for that matter."

"I'm not cut out for this." I shake my head.

"It will take some time to get used to it, but you will. I know this is not the most traditional way of getting married, but you are only delaying the inevitable."

"What do you mean?" I ask, surprised Mrs. Guerra thinks me marrying her son is a good idea.

"You've always wanted Leo. You loved him from the moment you met him. You have even learnt Italian for him."

"How do you know I still love him, and what makes you think I've learnt Italian?"

"Guerras are very good at reading people. We

have to be. And when that waiter apologised in Italian, you understood every word."

Not sure what to say, I let her continue.

"You will have a life of good fortune with the man you always wanted. The hows and the whys of all this are irrelevant, Katherine."

Truth be told, I've dreamed of a life with Leo, but this seems to be more like a nightmare. People say you should be careful what you wish for. I should have been more specific.

We finish our food and wine while making small talk. She was right—I did need to relax, and the wine has helped.

"Now let's get back to the dress shop and choose your wedding dress. I will have a word with Leo. He will not be choosing your dress; that is the bride's job."

Trying on wedding dresses is actually quite fun. Even though I don't plan on wearing the dress, I pick out a beautiful backless fitted gown.

After spending thousands of euros on Leo's card, we return to the house. Mrs. Guerra—or rather, Maria, as she has now insisted I call her —and I burst through the doors, a little tipsy and laughing hysterically. Not concentrating, I trip over the rug in the hall, and just as my knees are about smash into the marble floor, strong hands catch me and pull me against a hard, warm body.

Leo.

Chapter 15

Leo

Today I am in a bad mood. Yesterday I found out that Marco has been lying to me. Ever since I found Katherine all those years ago, living with a man I now know is her father, I have had Marco monitor her. Or so I thought. It seems Marco has decided that Katherine isn't the woman for me, so he has been withholding information from me and not monitoring her as I had asked. I am now questioning his loyalty.

To top that off, more of our cargo has been intercepted and stolen while crossing the ocean. Many men have been murdered in the process. Today was our biggest loss. Twenty loyal men have been slaughtered for the sake of a million euros' worth of cocaine. However, it's not really the product or the money value that interests me or the thieves; it's the power. They have stolen and got away with the Guerras' cargo. But not for long. I will have their heads on sticks.

Unfortunately, we aren't much closer to

discovering who these wannabes are. But we have found out that whoever is responsible is hacking into our IT system. This is how they get their information. At first I thought it was the Martelés. But after seeing the blood bath today, I know it is not their work. It's too chaotic. The Martelés have been in this game for generations. They are organised and precise like ourselves. These people are animals. Now that we know where their information comes from, we have set up a trap. We will be waiting. I have the best IT specialists money can buy. I will show them nobody steals from the Guerras.

Throughout the day, my fury escalates; my mind is racing, and my heart pounds in my chest. I feel like I'm letting my father and the Guerras down. So much guilt and frustration. But as soon as the front door opens, it disappears. Katherine is laughing with my mother. They are a little tipsy, each wearing the biggest smile. My mother hasn't smiled like this since before my brother died. Her smile reaches her eyes, and it's genuine joy. Katherine stumbles. My reaction is instant. I hold her in my arms as she regains her footing. My mother is still beaming with happiness as she watches us.

Katherine changes for dinner, and my day's trauma is soon forgotten. A black dress perfectly hugs the curves of her toned body. Something has changed in her tonight. It seems like she is flirting with me. She has sobered up a little since she arrived, but maybe it's still the alcohol controlling her. Her dress asks for attention. An intentional decision, I'm sure. I had wondered if I was a little harsh last night, but it seems all is forgiven—my mother's interference, I presume.

I listen to her make small talk while Alga serves our meal. Not missing her subtle flirtatious actions, I play dumb. When she pushes out her chest, I look down and take a mouthful of food. When her hand slightly brushes mine, I move it to lift my glass. I reply to her questions with one-word answers. The frustration starts to build inside her. The amusement threatens to show itself on my face, but I manage to keep it blank.

"Shall we have a drink outside, as it's a beautiful evening?" Katherine suggests.

"I've got some work to do, but you go ahead."

Her face is thunder. She stands up from the table and throws her napkin down. "I'm going to bed."

I let myself chuckle now she has left the room. I give her a few minutes and follow her into our bedroom.

She's surprised to see me. I close the door behind me and walk over to her. I'd guess that she's been pacing up and down in frustration. With each stride I take, she takes one step back until her back is against the wall. I continue walking until my body is against hers.

I bang the palm of my hand on the wall above her head. She jumps a little.

"What is the matter, Katherine?"

"Nothing." She turns her head away from me.

With my other hand, I take her jaw and gently turn it back to face me. I hold her gaze. "Do not lie to me. What is it you want?"

"You." She replies through a gasp.

She doesn't need to tell me again. My mouth connects with hers; she opens up for me. Her body melts into mine. It's like an explosion of old and new. She still tastes how I remember, sweet like a pineapple, her lips soft and plump. But there's a new confidence in her movements. Without separating our mouths, I lift her so she can wrap legs around me, and I carry her to the bed. After laying her down, I stand back and take in her beauty.

I remove my T-shirt and throw it aside. Katherine's eyes roam my body. She clearly likes what she sees. Crawling up to her, I take in her scent. Our mouths connect again, both equally hungry for each other. Her hands find my head and pull gently on my hair. Our bodies rock into each other, desperate for release. That won't be happening anytime soon. I have waited a long time for this. Plus, I told her I would make her beg, and beg she will. Guerras always keep their promises. I am about to show her just how much of a Guerra I am and how she will obey her husband.

Katie

My body is on fire. His touch is electric. It's like he is a pianist, and I am a piano. He knows just what key to press, how hard to press it. My mind and body are no longer mine; I can't resist him anymore.

He breaks our kiss; I miss him instantly until his lips move to my neck and down to my chest, kissing and tasting me as he goes. Moving down to my hips, he wastes no time in lifting my dress to my waist.

Sitting up to admire the small lace thong, he instructs, "Take them off. Show me how much you want me."

I comply immediately.

"Open wider," he growls like a predator.

The sound makes my hips buck. I need a release.

"You really do want me, don't you?"

"Yes. Please come here." I need to feel him on me.

"Not yet. I want to taste your impatience. Lie

back. Do not move."

His mouth connects with my clit, and I'm surprised it's not all over then. I've never been so desperate for anyone before. He's like this mixture of familiarity and comfort, danger and excitement. The sounds that come from my mouth surprise me. The growls Leo makes vibrate, adding to the sensation.

A little nip with his teeth, and I'm gone— no doubt alerting the whole house to my pleasure. As my orgasm calms, Leo does not. He continues massaging with his tongue. I'm so sensitive now that the way he flicks it has me bucking my hips. I feel the tips of his fingers join in, gently sliding up and down between my folds until I cry out.

"Ahhhh! Oooh." More pleasure fills me. Never have I ever had two orgasms so close together. I didn't think it was possible, but here we go again. I'm seeing stars, and tingles ripple through me; it's even better than the first.

"Leo, please—come here."

I need him in me now. I need his mouth on mine and his cock inside me. Leo ignores me and continues his work as if he hadn't just given me the two most amazing orgasms of my life. I can't take it much longer; I wiggle and squirm beneath him.

"Please, Leo, I need you inside me."

He continues, ignoring my plea.

"Leo... please...." I can barely speak with the euphoria.

This time he looks up, fingers still inside me as he says, "What do you want, Kat-er-een?"

"You.... Please, I need... you... inside."

He smiles. "I told you, you would beg for me."

Normally I'd be bothered by his smug face, knowing he was right, but at this moment in time, all I want is his—

Oh my god. HUGE!

Leo has removed his pants, and his heavy cock stands upright in front of me. *Wow.*

I pull my dress over my head and unclip my bra.

"On your knees."

I do as he says and feel him climb up the bed and kneel between my legs.

"Lift your ass and lower your shoulders."

I do, but obviously, not well enough, as a slap stings my bum. Wow, that was hot. I bend more deeply into position.

"Good girl." He rubs and soothes the area he just slapped.

The tip of his cock presses into my entrance. Slowly he stretches me as his head crowns. He wraps my hair around his fist and pulls it slightly and lifts my head.

"Tell me again what you want."

"You, Leo, I want you!" I cry as he quickly fills me like I've never been filled before.

"You feel that, Katherine? We were made for each other."

Oh my, do I feel that! It's incredible, the sensation of our bodies combined as one. Leo doesn't hold back; I didn't think he could go much deeper, but with each thrust, he does, and each time I'm closer and closer to orgasm number three. How does he do it?

"Come with me, Katherine!" His voice is raspy. He's ready.

I let go, feeling myself clench around him. We both explode together. The noises he makes and the way I feel make me want to cry. I slump down onto the bed in an emotional wreck. Leo does the same, his body covering mine.

"You were amazing."

His whisper makes me smile. Not that I did much to contribute, but I take the compliment anyway. After a few minutes of him smelling my hair and nibbling my ear, he removes himself and goes to the bathroom. I feel cold and empty in his absence, but I am too exhausted to move.

A few moments later, I'm being lifted off the

bed and placed into a warm bubble bath. Leo gets in, too, and places me on his lap. He lathers up a sponge and gently washes my body. I close my eyes as he massages my shoulders. I'm in heaven. After he's finished, Leo helps me out of the bath and wraps me in a big fluffy towel. We get into bed, and I settle on my side with my teddy, Snuggly.

"No, you sleep with me." He wraps his arm around my waist and pulls me in to spoon position with him behind me.

It feels good. Secure. I don't think I've ever been near anyone so dangerous, yet I feel the safest I ever have. Exhausted, I'm soon asleep.

When I wake, the bed is empty. There's a text from Leo on my phone, saying he will be back for lunch. Breakfast is laid out for me when I enter the kitchen.

"I hope you don't mind; I know you don't like to eat alone in the dining room, so as Mr. Guerra is out, I thought you might like to eat in here?" Alga looks worried, as if she may have done something wrong.

Quickly, I put her at ease. "Thank you, Alga; yes, I would much prefer to eat in here with you both."

Sergio is also in the kitchen, preparing something delicious as usual.

"There's an awful lot. Will you both join me?"

They both look at me.

"We've already eaten, but thank you for your kind offer." Alga declines.

Choosing the avocado and the smoked salmon, I make a bagel while chatting to the pair as they work. They tell me about their daughter, who is about my age. She has just qualified as a doctor. They are extremely proud, and listening to them talk about her is lovely. She has her graduation ceremony at the weekend; they're both extremely excited to see her wearing her cap and gown. Alga is worried they will embarrass her in front of her peers, but I assure them they definitely won't. I imagine they've worked very hard to get her to where she is. It makes me think of my parents, and I'm filled with homesickness.

The front door opens and closes, bringing me out of my thoughts. I hear the click of high heels on the marble floor. Interested to see who our visitor is, I go into the hallway and find Mia looking around.

"Hello, can I help you?"

Mia jumps, surprised to see me. "I'm looking for Marco, not that it's any of your business."

I really don't like this woman.

"I'm sorry, I vaguely remember meeting you

before, but I have forgotten your name?" I say, even though I haven't.

"It's Mia," she reminds me displeased.

"Mia—ahh, yes. Do you always let yourself into other people's homes without knocking?" I fold my arms across my chest.

She scowls back at me. "I'm always welcome here; I'm practically family."

"Well, as I live here now, I would greatly appreciate it if you would knock in the future."

"Ha, I don't think that is necessary. You are forgetting your place."

My blood boils.

"No, I think you are forgetting yours, Mia. I am Mrs.-Guerra-to-be, and I am sure my fiancé, Mr. Guerra, would agree that we don't want just anyone walking into our home where we may be in situations that we don't want people to see. Do you understand?"

She's furious. Her left eye starts to twitch. I have to contain my laugh. I can hear sniggers coming from the kitchen. No doubt Alga and Sergio are listening.

"I will speak to Leo about you," she spits.

"Please be my guest, but remember to knock when you do."

I swear I see steam coming out of her nose.

Before she can say anything in return, Marco appears from Leo's office.

"Ladies."

"Chi crede di essere?" Who does she think she is? Mia mutters to Marco. *Who does she think she is?*

Marco turns to me and smirks.

"A Guerra." He winks at me, then escorts Mia out.

Ha, silly cow.

Chapter 16

Katie

"Marco, would you be able to drive me into town? I need to pick up a few things."

He nods and grabs his keys. Looks like we are going now. I follow quickly before he changes his mind. We quickly arrive downtown.

The last time we were here, I spotted a little beauty shop. It's not like the wholesalers we have at home, but I'm sure I'll be able to get what I need. After speaking to Alga this morning, I want to make her feel better about attending her daughter's graduation. I think a hair makeover will really make her feel better about herself. I'm in my element, walking around the shop, picking out new brushes, clips, and scissors. It's not the quality I use at home, but they'll do the job. Only thinking I was going on holiday, I didn't bring my hairdressing kit, just my electricals and a few bits I need to do my own hair.

Marco follows me around, groaning as I pick up every item for a good look. I get what I need for Alga's hair as well as some new bits for me. My basket is pretty full when I get to the counter.

"No charge," the lady says, looking directly at Marco.

"What? No, please—these are for me." I get everything out of the basket and hold out my bank card.

"No charge, please."

I look from this woman to Marco, feeling extremely uncomfortable.

"Let her pay," Marco instructs.

Without looking at me, she scans the items and holds out the payment machine. I tap my card and pick up my bag, feeling very deflated.

In the car on the way back to the house, I can see Marco looking at me through the rearview mirror.

"You will get used to it."

I don't say anything in return. I don't want to get used to it.

When we get back, I set up a salon area in our bathroom. The bathroom is huge, with plenty of room for the chair I bring in from the dressing table. There's lots of worktop space for all my colouring products and tools; there's even a sprayer that pulls out on the sink to wash her hair.

Filled with excitement, I go and get Alga.

"I've got a surprise for you; come with me." I beckon Alga to follow me.

"A surprise for me?"

"Yes, come on. You'll be okay without her for a couple of hours, won't you, Sergio?"

"Of course, you girls go." He waves us out of the kitchen.

I take Alga into the bathroom.

"If it's okay with you, Alga, I'd like to do your hair."

Alga looks around at my makeshift salon, shocked.

"Oh no, I can't; I have to work, Mr. Guerra…."

"Mr. Guerra will be fine. Please, it will make me happy."

"I can't afford it."

"Don't be silly—it's my treat. Now sit."

I walk her to the chair and put a gown around her before she can argue any more. I position her in front of the mirror and take out her bobble. Alga has always worn her hair tied up in a tight, high bun. I guessed it would be long, but I didn't realise how long. Her hair is dark with strands of grey running through it. It's all different lengths and wispy. I'd guess she hasn't had it cut professionally in many years.

"How do you feel about your hair, Alga?

Are you attached to the length, or would you be prepared to go to this sort of length?" I gesture with my hands just below her shoulders. About seven inches would be coming off the longest sections if she agrees.

"Do whatever you like; I trust you." She nods and smiles, and I can tell she does.

"Great. We will give you some layers as well, frame your face; it will really suit you. I was thinking of keeping your natural dark-and-silver hair, but I'll do some highlights and low lights, then a toner, to give it some more definition.

"Yes, yes, whatever you think."

"Wonderful."

I waste no time in getting started. I'm really enjoying doing what I love. I've missed this. While I'm working my magic, we talk and laugh. It's lovely to see Alga like this, relaxed and being looked after rather than her doing all the work.

Once the colour is done and I've finished the restyle cut, I blow-dry her hair bouncy with a bit of curl. I purposely face her away from the mirror until I am finished. I must admit, it does look pretty amazing. I love doing transformations like this. Alga looks at least ten years younger. Her sparse, dull, lifeless hair is now thick, shiny, and full of style.

I spin her chair around so she faces the

mirror. For a moment, she doesn't say a word, and I worry she doesn't like it. But then tears fill her eyes as she touches her new bouncy locks.

"Is this me?" she cries.

"You look beautiful, Alga."

"Thank you."

"What's going on in here?!" Leo demands as he storms into the bathroom.

Alga jumps from her seat and rips the gown from around her neck.

Chapter 17

Katie

"I have just done Alga's hair; doesn't she look amazing?" I beam.

Leo looks from me to her.

"Alga and Sergio's daughter graduates as a doctor this weekend. Isn't that amazing?"

"Alga… you look…. lovely," he says, plainly, and I'm unable to read his thoughts. He then leaves, closing the door behind him.

Alga looks like she's in shock. She gazes at herself in the mirror again.

"Thank you so much."

"You're very welcome. Come on—let's go and show Sergio, see what he thinks."

Alga beams; I follow her to the kitchen.

Sergio loves Alga's hair, and quite rightly so. He grabs her by the waist and spins her around, doing a little dance.

"Sergio!" Leo's bellowing voice makes us all

jump.

"Sì, Signor Guerra."

"Kat-er-een informs me your daughter is graduating as a doctor."

A proud look comes over Sergio's face. "Sì."

Leo holds out an envelope, and after a few seconds, Sergio takes it.

"A gift; send her our congratulations." He then holds out another to Alga.

"A thank you for your hard work and loyalty."

Leo then exits the room, leaving a very shocked-looking Alga and Sergio in his wake. They both open their envelopes and pull out a cheque. Gasps and little squeals come from their mouths.

I leave them to their excitement and go find Leo. He's in his office, typing away on his computer.

"That was a lovely thing you just did."

"They've worked for our family ever since I can remember; I never knew they had a daughter."

I'm not surprised he didn't know that. I don't comment; I can tell from his face that he is annoyed at himself for this.

"I'm going to have some lunch. Are you joining me?"

"I'm not hungry."

He's in his work mode, so I leave him to it. Just as I'm about the close the door behind me, he speaks up.

"On second thoughts, I wouldn't mind a little taste of something. Come, sit." He pushes back from his desk and taps his lap.

The look he gives me with the raised eyebrow and smirk on his lips has me obeying immediately. I go to sit sideways, but he turns me to straddle him. He pulls me by my bum into him so I can feel his hardness at my heat. His mouth is on mine, and I realise I've missed him terribly since this morning. We devour each other as if consuming our last meal. My body automatically grinds against him. He pushes himself against me harder. The pressure has me moaning.

"Not yet." He lifts me off him and sits me on his desk. "Take them off."

I pull my little shorts off along with my thong as quickly as I can.

He smiles. "Good girl. Now spread those legs as wide as you can. Let me see all your beauty."

Being quite flexible, I can spread my legs pretty far apart. He raises an eyebrow, impressed with my efforts.

"Very nice." He unzips and pushes his pants to the floor. His cock springs to attention, all smooth and hard.

"Put me inside of you." He stands in between my legs.

I take hold of him. My hand is too small to close around his girth. I guide him to my entrance, but then rub the tip against my clit, then down to my wetness and back up again.

"That's it. You're so beautiful."

And he really makes me feel it. I repeat the movement a few times, both of us letting out a little groan. Then I insert him, feeling myself stretch around his smooth, round tip.

"Are you ready?"

"Yes," I gasp.

"I want your eyes on mine at all times." His hands find my waist as he thrusts, filling and stretching me, making us one again. I throw my head back automatically as I moan through the pleasure.

"Eyes on me!"

I quickly return his gaze. His eyes are dark, his brows furrowed. For the next goodness knows how many minutes, we are in a world of our own, pleasuring each other immensely and rewarding each other in return with emotions through our gaze. We are on fire. Our bodies are connected, working in sync. If someone walked into the room right now, I don't think either of us would notice.

Our climaxes come at the same time. Together we shake and pulse.

Holding each other afterward like we never want to let go, we let our heartbeats calm and our breathing turn shallow. He kisses my ear and whispers into it again, and I think I love this bit as much as the rest.

When we've finally given in and are now dressed, Marco knocks on the door.

"Entrare." *Enter.*

They don't say a word to each other; they just nod as if they can speak telepathically.

"I'll leave you to work."

Leo kisses my forehead, and I leave the room, closing the door behind me.

The next day I go and visit Emmaline and Alfie. Alfie's doing great. Completely back to normal. Macy greets me excitedly at the door, recognising me immediately, barking at me to stroke her. Once we're inside the house, Emmaline makes us each a cup of tea, and we sit at the table. Alfie goes outside and plays chase with Macy.

"So, the word on the street is, you are soon to be the next Mrs. Guerra."

"Oh, don't remind me." I put my head in my hands.

"What exactly is the situation, Katie?"

"Where do I start?"

I've not known Emmaline for long, and although I feel I can trust her, I don't want to offload everything onto her. Plus, knowing things about the Guerras could prove dangerous. I tell her the bare minimum, leaving out the contract and how I've been threatened with legal action and goodness knows what else if I don't comply.

Thinking about Leo and our relationship now, I realise they're both so different from when I first arrived. Maybe if I spoke to him, he would call off the wedding, and we could just date and see how things go. If only that part could be different too. I'm starting to fall in love with him again. Or maybe I never stopped. But this life he leads? I can't see myself in it. Yesterday in the shop, that woman wouldn't let me pay. She was scared. I don't want people to feel like that around me. The night at the opera, people had shot at Leo just because of who he is. I don't belong in that life; I don't want that life. Maybe Leo knows that, and that's why he has arranged this ludicrous wedding.

"I suppose in a weird way, and if he wasn't some mobster, it might be quite romantic." Emmaline admits.

"Yeah, I suppose it would."

"Do you want to marry him?"

I can't answer that question.

"Leo is...." I begin, but I'm saved by Alfie coming in and demanding a drink. After that, I manage to keep the conversation away from mine and Leo's relationship, but I can't keep my mind from going there as easily.

At dinner that night, Leo seems more relaxed.

"I heard you had a discussion of sorts with Mia today?" Leo asks sarcastically.

"You could say that. Who is she, anyway, and why does she think she can just walk in?"

"She's the daughter of my father's number one."

"I know that, but why does she just walk into your home? Have you two had a relationship? Or are you still in a relationship?" The question makes me sick to my stomach.

"Katherine, I am a loyal man. I can promise you that as long as you are with me, I will only be with you. That stands for you also. I am very protective over what belongs to me. Do you understand? You are mine now, only mine."

He strokes the side of my face and kisses my forehead, then continues. "With regard to Mia letting herself in, she and Marco have something going on between them. I'm not sure what; I've never asked; that's his business. Though I doubt after your little performance today, she will walk in unannounced again." He chuckles.

I love when he is happy like this. I decide now is a good time to ask about the wedding.

Chapter 18

Katie

"Leo, I want to speak to you about the wedding."

He puts down his knife and fork and straightens in his chair.

"Hear me out, please. Just let me say what I need to before you say anything."

"I'm listening."

"Could we postpone the wedding for a while?"

He grunts.

"We can stay engaged and just get to know each other more. I've always had feelings for you, Leo, and there's something amazing growing between us. Forcing all this will only ruin us. Why can't we have a relationship like normal people? Let me introduce you to my family; let them get to know you before we get married?"

I can see his brain ticking over what I'm saying, so I keep going. "And that contract, do we really need that?"

He rubs his chin as if considering what I've just said. <u>Before</u> he can answer, Marco bursts through the door.

"Tuo padre." *Your father.*

Leo stands up, and they both quickly leave the room.

"Katherine, you're coming too!" Leo shouts from the hallway.

I guess I'm going as well.

On the way to the hospital, Leo looks extremely worried. I don't know what to expect when we get there, and I'm too afraid to ask. His hand is on the seat beside me. I put my hand over his and give him a little squeeze. He doesn't respond, just continues looking straight ahead.

When we get to the hospital, we are shown to a room where his mother waits outside. Her face is red and puffy.

"Leo." His mother hugs him. "Katherine, thank you for coming." She hugs me too.

"How is he?"

"Not good; come sit with him." Maria opens the door.

"Do you want to come in, Katherine?"

"No, thank you, Maria. You two go ahead. I'll get us some coffee."

Leo nods at Marco, instructing him to come with me. I roll my eyes. I didn't notice on the way in, but the hallway leading up to the room is well-guarded by Guerra men. They all look as mean as each other. Each one nods at me as I walk past them. When I get to the café to get the coffee, my phone rings; it's my dad.

"Hi, Dad!" It's so great to hear his voice.

"Hi, Love, how are you? Are you enjoying your holiday?"

"I'm great, Dad, yeah. Hey, you remember years ago when I met that boy on holiday with Mum?"

"Oh yeah—Leo, was it? The one whose name you had all over your schoolbooks. You had me searching the internet for him at the library at one point." He laughs.

That's true; I'd forgotten about that.

"Well, you'll never guess who I've bumped into while here."

"No! You've finally found him, have you?"

More like he found me.

"Yes, I have."

"Well, I'm pleased for you, love; I know you always wondered what happened to him. You were quite taken by him, weren't you."

"I was," I agree.

"What is he like? Is he still a teenage heartthrob, or is he fat and bald now?" Dad laughs at his own joke.

"He's definitely not fat and bald, but he's a bit different than I imagined."

"Oh yeah? How so?" Dad asks, concerned.

"Oh, you know, just different; he's the boss of a big business now—a lot different from the teenage boy I remember." That's an understatement.

"I'm sure. Well, you just enjoy yourself, love. When do you come home? I don't remember you saying when your flight was?"

"I've not booked one yet."

"Oh, it's all right for some, having long holidays. Well, don't stay there too long; I miss that face of yours. Take care, love. Speak soon."

"Yeah, speak soon, Dad; love you."

"Love you, too, Katie."

I slump down in a chair and put my head in my hands. I miss my dad. I hated lying to him then, but if I have to go through with this wedding, I need him there. It will still be a shock with how quickly it is happening, but at least I have planted the seed now. Taking a deep breath, I get up and join the queue for the drinks. When we return to the waiting room, I hand Marco a coffee, take mine from the tray, and leave Leo's and Maria's beside me.

"Leo, you don't need to do this," Maria disagrees, as she and Leo re-join us.

"There's no discussion. We will bring the wedding forward to this weekend."

What? Wait, did I just hear him right?

I grab the coffees off the table and hand them out, trying to make sense of the situation. Maria takes hers with thanks, but Leo just stares at the cup, not taking it from my hand.

"What's going on? How is your dad?" I ask.

The face of the man in front of me is not my Leo but the face of the leader of the Guerras. It is expressionless.

"The wedding is to be moved forward to this weekend."

"No, please, Leo—that's only days away."

"My decision is final. Marco, make the necessary arrangements."

Leo takes hold of my hand, holding tightly at my wrist. "Kat-er-een , we are going home." He pulls me out of the room and through the hospital. We get in the car and are soon joined by Marco, who climbs into the front seat and starts the engine.

"What is happening, Leo? Is your father dying?"

He shuts me down. "Do not disrespect me, Katherine."

I am furious. He is so used to people backing down and doing everything he says; well, not this time. I will not be his puppet. I ignore him all the way back to the house. As soon as we stop, I am out of the car, not waiting for anyone to open my door. Storming through the house, I get a few stares from the house workers. Leo is calling me in the distance, asking me to wait, but I disobey him. After going into my room and locking the door behind me, I get my phone out and ring Damien.

He answers on the first ring. "Katie, how are you?"

"Going crazy. Listen, Damien, Leo wants to bring the wedding forward to this weekend. You have to help me."

"It's almost done. There's no way he can force you into this; we have him in so many ways. The main one being that you no longer use the name Katherine. You go by Katie; your bank accounts all have Katie as the name, and so does your driving licence. The letter you wrote, saying you would marry him was signed with the name Katherine. That is no longer you. Legally you can walk away; I just need to ensure there are no comebacks. Once we get you to England, there's nothing he can do. Hang tight; we have a plan. You will be home by the weekend."

"Oh, I hope so, Damien."

"Stay safe; I will see you soon."

Just as I end the call, Leo bangs on the door.

"Katherine, Let me in now!"

"No. Go away."

Crash. Leo kicks the door, breaking the lock, and it swings open. I sit on the bed with my back to him, pretending to be unfazed.

"Why are you ignoring me?"

I stand up and go to walk out of the door.

He grabs my elbow as I pass. "Do not walk away from me."

My eyes snap to his, a dare for him to challenge me. A smirk rises on his lips.

"Oh, dear Katherine. Do not tempt me."

"Urgh." I shrug out of his hold, trying to cover up the reaction of my body to his words. He's quicker than I am. He makes it to the door first, slamming the broken latch back into the door frame.

I reach for the handle to pull it open, but he spins me around so my back is against the door. With his body pressed against mine, one hand takes my jaw, and the other leans on the door above my head.

"I don't like to be disobeyed. You need to

learn to respect the Guerras."

"In that case, you need to respect me."

His eyebrow rises.

"If I am to be a Guerra, you need to show me some more respect."

"I will not have you arguing with me in front of people on my payroll."

"Fine, I will save it for here. Respect is earned, Leo. You have earned none from me."

"What do you mean?"

"You are forcing me into a marriage. Threatening me with goodness knows what if I don't."

"I have only brought forward the inevitable. What is the point of waiting? We have wasted enough time apart already." He trails kisses along my jaw, making my frustration disperse.

Is what he says true? If I had a choice, would I marry him in time anyway? It is what my teenage dreams were always made of. Leo and I married, spending the rest of our lives together, living in a vineyard in Italy. It is my dream come true, only with a few major additions. I really should have been more specific.

"But it isn't what I want."

"Oh, it is. Look at how your body reacts to me." He strokes his fingers down my arms.

Goosebumps cover my skin in their wake. "You belong to me, Katherine. You just need to let your mind listen to your body. It knows what it wants. Me."

His mouth crashes into mine. Mine automatically opens up to him. He's right; my body is controlled by him. It has no mind of its own.

"No." I break the kiss and push him away, much to the disappointment of my body.

Leo takes a step back. His eyes are dark, with a small smirk on one side of his lips. "Stop fighting this, Katherine. You need to listen to your body."

Stepping forward again, leaning his body into mine, he grabs both my wrists and holds them above my head with one hand. He does it so quickly that I gasp. With his other hand, he undoes his tie. He then wraps the tie around my wrists, locking them together.

"Just relax. Trust your body, your instincts."

You'd think my instincts would be telling me to fight, to run. I've just been restrained, but my body is hot and tingling in anticipation of his next move. He then pulls on the tie, making my arms stretch up. It's not uncomfortable, but it has really restricted my movements. He fastens the tie to a hook on the back of the door.

"Perfect." Standing back, he takes in my whole body, which is now warm and needy.

He wanders into his wardrobe and returns with another tie. It's made of black silk. He strokes it over my skin—my arms, my chest, my neck. It feels incredible. He watches each stroke with such concentration, as if he is painting a masterpiece. His mouth takes mine again; my body melts into him. I hear myself moan and my breathing picks up. The silk moves up my neck and covers my eyes. He ties it at the back of my head. I break the kiss. Everything is pitch-black.

Just as I'm about to panic, Leo holds my face, his mouth at my ear. "Just relax. Let your other senses take over. Your hearing, smell, touch. Trust your body."

Then he leaves me. I sense he is still in the room. The sound of him undressing to my left catches my attention. I can hear him open each button on his shirt. The sound of the fabric sliding over his shoulders and arms. The connection of the different materials as it lands on the chair he throws it on. The unbuckling of his belt. A zip being unfastened. Material against the skin and hair on his legs. All that as well as the sound of my breathing, which is deeper and louder, and my heart. which pounds in anticipation. My nose tingles with the smell of his aftershave as it gets stronger. He's coming closer.

He unhooks my hands from the door and places them around his neck. I search for his mouth with my lips; it's as hungry as mine is.

Fingertips trail down my arms onto my shoulders. The hairs on my skin stand to attention, and a little shiver ripples through my body. His fingers find the zip on the back of my dress. The lack of straps means he can easily remove it from my body. I step out of the dress while he holds me steady, my arms still around his neck.

I lean into him. I'm met with the most intoxicating warmth. I melt into him, trying to touch his skin with as much of mine as I can. He guides us away from the door. He arranges my body so I'm straddling a chair, my arms still tied and hooked over the back of it. I feel his lack of presence while I hear him in the bathroom. When he returns, his hands cover my shoulders and begin to massage me. A moan leaves my lips as I feel all my tension melt away. His thumbs work magic up the vertebrae in my neck, releasing knots and loosening my movements. The smell of coconut from the oil he rubs on my skin, mixed with the smell of Leo, makes my mouth water. The sound of our moans as we appreciate each other's bodies fuels my need to touch him, to taste him.

His hands move down my arms; I push back as he comes closer to me. "I need you, Leo."

"I know you do." He lifts me off the chair and places me on the bed. He lays his body over mine. My hips buck, searching for the release it craves. My heat finds his hard length, and I wrap my legs around him, squeezing him into me.

"My desperate girl. I said you wanted me. I know your body better than you know it yourself."

It's true. My body betrays all logic, all common sense. It wants him, only him, and it wants him so badly, I think I may cry if he doesn't take me right now. He pulls away, and my body instantly tries to find him. It doesn't need to search far. He is knelt in between my legs, removing my thong. I spread wide for him. The groan of appreciation he makes spurs me on more.

I rise up, wrapping myself around him once more. "Untie me; I want to touch you."

He rips the tie from my hands, then removes the blindfold. It's like he's released an animal. I'm up and on him, forcing him back onto the bed. I hold his arms down and kiss him. Taste him. I rub myself up his length before lifting up and pushing down so intensely that we both moan in pleasure. I rise up and grind. I kiss his mouth and bite his lips. I suck his nipples and nip them between my teeth.

His moans and facial expression encourage me to work harder to give us both the most intense pleasure. It builds between us. The joining of our bodies is tight, hot, and wet, and I never want to break this connection. It builds and builds. We both thrust and shake uncontrollably. He slaps my bum and holds my hips down as he uses the last of his energy to intensify our orgasms. A scream I have no control over leaves my throat. Leo's eyes never leave mine. I know in that moment I belong to him. There's nothing I can do to stop it. My body is his. He has claimed me.

The next day, I go to the beach to gather my thoughts. I feel incredible. Every inch of my body aches with love. We spent all last night getting to know and love every part of each other's body. There's not one scar or freckle on Leo's body that I haven't kissed.

"Hey, what are you looking happy about?" Emmaline comes and sits next to me on the blanket I have laid out on the sand.

"Oh, nothing, really," I tell her. "How are you all?"

"We are all good, thanks to your fiancé. I owe him so much, which is a little scary, considering he is who he is."

"Don't worry, Leo doesn't hold that kind of debt against people."

Emmaline smiles and nods, but neither of us speaks again for a while. We both know what kind of debt Leo does hold against people and what he does to those people when he collects.

We watch Alfie and Macy dog play on the shore Macy's white fur grows browner from rolling around in the wet sand as Alfie chuckles away at the puppy's mischief. Emmaline and I make small talk until I hear my name being called in the distance. At first, I don't recognise the voice, so I ignore it, thinking there must be another Katie on the beach, but as it gets louder, the prickles on the back of my neck have me searching for where the sound is coming from. A large male figure walks towards us, waving his hands.

"Katie!" the man booms.

He's so loud, most of the beach looks at him. Although I can't quite make out his face, I recognise the swagger in his walk. Jax. What the hell is he doing here?

Chapter 19

Katie

"Do you know that guy, Katie?"

My jaw drops open. He is the very last person I expect to see on his beach. A hundred things run through my mind. What is he doing here? When did he get out of prison? How did he know where I am? Has he been looking for me? Oh god, what will Leo do if he sees me talking to him?

"Umm, sorry, Emmaline—I'm just a little shocked. Yes, I know him. It's my ex-boyfriend."

"Ohh, tricky; I'll leave you to it."

Emmaline leaves just as Jax approaches, and I stand up.

"Katie!" Jax wraps his arms around me. I don't hug him back, so he releases me.

"What are you doing here, Jax?"

"Well, that's not the reaction I was expecting; I was released from prison a few days ago. I went looking for you but was told you'd gone on holiday. So here I am." He opens his arms with a big cheesy grin, like I should just melt into his arms.

"Why didn't you call me?"

"I wanted to surprise my girl."

Oh god, he doesn't think we are still together, does he?

"Jax, I didn't know what was happening or what had happened to you. I wasn't sure if I would ever see you again."

"I didn't know what was happening either. I'm sorry, babe. I should have called you, but all I could think of was seeing your face." He strokes my cheek. "I was framed, babe. They finally saw sense and let me go. All I've thought about is you. I can't believe I'm finally here with you. I've missed you so much."

Guilt grips my stomach. He goes to hold my hand, but I pull away. He has been in prison all this time for something he hasn't done. He thought his girlfriend was waiting for him on the outside, but instead, I was here with Leo.

Jax is a typically attractive man. But he does nothing for me anymore. Not like the tingles I get from Leo just from hearing him say my name.

"Katherine!"

There they are; it's like my skin physically hears him. Oh, dear. I'm scared for Jax. I turn to meet him.

"Leo, hi."

One of his spies has obviously alerted him to Jax's presence.

Both Leo and Jax are similar in height and build, but I know Leo will kill Jax in one swift movement.

"This is a friend of mine—Jax." I gesture to Jax.

"Friend?" Jax asks, clearly perplexed.

"Jaxon Adams?" Leo queries. I shouldn't be surprised that Leo knows who he is, but I am.

"Guerra," Jax replies.

Okay, do they know each other? The men puff out their chests and shoulders. Both their stares could kill.

"We are leaving, Katherine." Leo beckons.

Jax looks at me in question.

"Jax, it's great to see you. But I have plans right now. Can I catch up with you later?"

"I suppose." He looks upset, and I feel terrible.

"You still have the same mobile number?"

"Yep." He waves his phone at me.

"Great, speak soon," I shout back as Leo pulls me away, grunting.

He doesn't speak to me the whole way back,

just mutters under his breath. When we get to the house, he lets go of my hand and goes into his office. I take a deep breath and follow him. He pours himself a drink, downs it, and pours another. He then goes to his desk, pulls out a cigar, lights it, and sits down. I feel like I'm in serious trouble.

"Jaxon Adams?" Leo questions, as if the name hurts him.

"Yes, how do you know him?"

"I told you; I make it my business to know whom my wife-to-be has recently been around. What is he doing here?"

"Well, I'm not quite sure; you pulled me away before I had the chance to speak to him," I answer sarcastically.

"I will not have other men touching my wife!" He slams his hand on his desk.

I keep my composure. "Calm down. There's no need for this."

He squeezes his hands to fists in anger.

"Firstly, I am not your wife, and secondly, he was hardly touching me; he just gave me a hug, as he was pleased to see me."

He sits back in his chair and takes a long drag on his cigar.

"Look, I don't know how much you know

about him, but I'm going to tell you the truth. Jax and I were in a relationship before I came here."

Leo's eye twitches, he forcefully blows out his smoke.

"He was arrested days before I left for something he didn't even do. The reason I came here was because some guys came round to his house, and Jax told me to leave and not return. I thought these guys were following me, and I panicked. That's why I accepted your plane ticket. I needed to get away."

Leo sits forward in his chair as he demands, "What guys? What did they look like?"

Hold on a minute. Is Leo the reason Jax was in prison?

"Did you frame Jax?"

"He doesn't love you." He drains his drink, stands up, and pours another.

"It was you, wasn't it!? Seriously Leo, have you been controlling my whole life?" I'm furious. My breathing is erratic. My heartbeat pounds in my ears.

"Do you love him?" Leo demands, making me jump a little.

The answer to that question is easy. No, I don't love Jax. I don't think I ever did. But for some reason, I say...

"Yes."

Crash. His glass hits the wall to the side of me. There's pain in his eyes, and I instantly regret that tiny word. I'm just about to beg for forgiveness and tell him the truth when he opens the safe behind him and throws my passport at me. "Get the fuck out!"

He means it. He looks like he wants to kill me. I leave. I run to my room, throw everything into my case as quickly as possible, and make my way to the front door. Marco stands in front of it. He doesn't say a word, just winks and lets me pass. I run down the driveway as fast as I can before he changes his mind. I wonder whether Jax was sent by Damien, that this was the way to get me home. Either way, I'm finally free, finally going home. A taxi drives by, so I wave it down. As soon as I'm inside it, I ring Jax.

"Hi, Jax, it's me. Where are you?"

"Katie, sooner than I thought. I'm in a bar near the beach where you left me."

"I'll pick you up in two minutes; that okay?" I ask hopefully.

"Sure." He seems surprised, but pleased I won't be long.

Two minutes later, Jax joins me in the taxi, and we are on our way to the airport.

"Are you sure you don't need to pick

anything up?" I ask.

"No, I only brought this bag. You're all I need. But did you manage to pack everything?" Jax seems concerned.

"I hope so. I just shoved everything into my case. It doesn't matter if I didn't; I suppose I can buy new," I reply.

"What about that scruffy of yours?"

"Snuggly? My teddy? Yeah, he's safely in my bag." I tap my handbag beside me.

Jax smiles and laughs. "If there's one thing I can always rely on, it's that you will have that thing with you wherever you go."

Still laughing, he pulls me into a side hug. I try to ignore his use of the word "thing" when referring to my teddy. He knows how important he is to me.

When we arrive at the airport, Jax gets out of his side and closes the taxi door. After a moment or two, I realise he isn't coming back to open my door. Jax never has done, though. I have become used to Leo opening my door and helping me out. I feel a pang in my chest as I think of him. Taking a deep breath, I open my door, pay the taxi driver, and follow Jax into the airport.

There's a flight leaving in thirty minutes.

"If you hurry, you will make it before the gate closes." The lady at the check in desk points us in the right direction.

We run through passport control and get on the plane just before they close the gate. I slump into my seat beside Jax. The flight attendants close the plane doors and start their safety checks.

"So, Jax, how are you? What have the police said? Did they find out who framed you?"

Jax is messaging someone on his phone. He holds it at an angle so I can't see the screen.

"Jax?"

He's abrupt when he responds, "Just give me a minute."

I'm surprised by his tone. Maybe he is stressed and doesn't want to talk about prison. I give him a few minutes to finish his messages. The flight attendant comes around to check our seat belts.

"Could you put your phone on flight mode now, please, sir?"

"In a minute," Jax snaps back.

"I'm sorry, sir, but it's very important that you turn it off right now so as not to interfere with the aircraft's communication for takeoff."

"Right, right, it's off. Happy now?" He puts his phone in his pocket.

I have never heard him be so rude before.

"Is everything okay?" I ask, concerned.

"It's fine. I'm just tired. Do you mind just letting me get some rest?" He puts in his earphones, lays his head back, and closes his eyes.

I'm confused. He comes all the way to Italy to find me the minute he gets released from prison, but as soon as we have time together, he wants to sleep? Maybe it was Damien who arranged for him to come and get me. At least I am going home. Back to England, rainy England. Back to work. Back to my lonely apartment.

Oh no, what have I done? My heart feels heavy at the thought of being so far away from Leo. The last time I saw him, he was so hurt. I did that to him. He'd better not do anything stupid. I get out my phone to message him but then remember it's on flight mode. As soon as we land, I will send him a message.

The next two hours and twelve minutes drag like you wouldn't believe. I have read the inflight magazines front to back I don't know how many times. I've had drinks and snacks and played stupid games that I didn't even know I had on my phone, and Jax still has his earphones in, sat in the same position.

The minute we start to leave the plane, I switch my phone on. It instantly rings. Bella lights up my screen.

"Bella, I've just landed; I'm home!"

Jax turns around, annoyed. "Get off the

phone," he mouths angrily.

I'm not sure why. There were plenty of other people on their phones, and the cabin crew didn't say anything as I walked past them.

"You have? Already? Damien said you would be home in a couple of days. I was ringing to arrange to meet up."

So maybe Damien didn't arrange for Jax to get me, or maybe hasn't told Bella everything.

"Great, well, it's getting late now. I think Jax mentioned a taxi picking us up from the airport, but it will take at least an hour or so. How about tomorrow morning?"

"You're with Jax?" Her tone seems worried.

"Yeah, he surprised me, so we came home together."

"You know, he came looking for you at the salon a day or two after you left. I said I didn't know where you were, but that you had gone on holiday. He got quite angry, actually. We had to get security to escort him out."

"Really? That doesn't sound like him. Not long after I left, did you say?"

"Yes, like the day after."

This doesn't make sense; Jax said he only just got out.

"Oh, okay. I need to speak to him. I'll catch

you up with everything tomorrow. So, meet you at our usual cafe?"

"Perfect. I can't wait to see you; I'm dying to hear all your news. Text me when you're safely home, and I'll see you tomorrow."

"Will do. See you tomorrow."

I'm so looking forward to seeing Bella. I wonder how much Damien has explained to her. I'll tell her the whole truth now. Just as I'm about to put my phone back in my bag, Jax snatches it off me.

"Hey!"

"I need to borrow it to ring the taxi; I have no signal."

Not wanting to argue, I let him take it. He's very off. I wonder whether he's annoyed at me for being in Italy with Leo. Jax was probably expecting a big welcome from me, which he didn't get.

At baggage claim, my case is one of the first off the carousel. Perks of being the last one on, I suppose.

"Jax, I'm all set."

Jax has been oblivious to me retrieving my case and standing beside him. He's not stopped messaging on his phone since we landed. So much for needing mine, as he had no signal.

"Let's go." He takes off at speed.

I follow, trying to keep up. I think of Leo and how different he would be in this situation. Although the Don of an incredibly powerful organisation, he is a true gentleman. Leo would have retrieved my case. He would carry it— or rather, pull it along—for me; he would stay walking at my side, open every door, and take care of me. I miss him.

I need my phone.

"Jax! Wait up, I need my phone!"

"Come on, the taxis here; we need to hurry!"

He walks even faster now. We practically run through arrivals and out of the doors. The cool English air hits my lungs; I take a deep breath and look up to the night sky, where the stars are twinkling. *I'm home*, I think, as raindrops hammer onto my face.

"Katie! Come on this way!" Jax is disappearing off to the right and down a dark path.

"Jax, but it says taxis this way!"

"No, it's parked round here; come on!"

I hope it's not far. I'm starting to get wet through. I've not missed this rain.

As I hurry down a dark alley, it smells of rubbish and stale smoke; I follow Jax's shadow. He turns left at the end. Keeping my head down so I don't to get rain in my eyes, I, too, turn left. My head hits a hard chest.

"Oh, I'm so sorry!" I can tell the man I have just run into isn't Jax. But before I can lift my head to see his face, a hood is placed over mine, and my hands are held behind my back.

"No need to apologise," the man says in an Italian accent.

My case is removed from my hand, and the bag from my arm. My hands are then fastened together. I'm lifted over someone's shoulder, carried a few steps, and then thrown into what I guess is the back of a van.

My bum hits the hard floor; a pain shoots straight up my back. "Ouch."

There's no point fighting this. I've just spent weeks with the Guerras; I know I'll not win. It's The Guerras. I should have known Leo wouldn't just let me come home. He's let me get all the way back to England, then kidnapped me. He wouldn't hurt me, though, would he?

I wince when the van starts to move, and I'm flung back. Or maybe he would; they're not exactly being gentle with me. He must be so mad. I wonder if they'll take me straight back to Italy or if Leo is here. Jax must be worried sick. He'll wonder where I am. Unless he saw what happened and has rung the police? But maybe he won't want to do that, having just been wrongly accused by them.

But *was* he wrongly accused? Nothing makes sense anymore. There's something off with

Jax. Why did he say he'd only just gotten out? And why would he not want to talk to me? I should have just stayed in Italy. What trouble have I gotten into now? The drive seems to go on for hours, but it's probably only about one hour. I'm furious with Leo for this; he could have easily talked me into going back. I was already missing him. Why does he keep spoiling something that could be good? Hopefully, one day he will realise we could have had this dream for real.

The door opens with a squeak. Loud footsteps echo towards me on the metal floor.

"Get up."

An arm hooks through mine and pulls me up and forward. Feeling him jump out of the vehicle, I do the same, but my foot catches on something, and I fall. Unable to put my hands out in front of me, my knees hit the ground with a crunch. My left kneecap shatters on the hard gravel.

"Arhhh!" I scream, unable to hold in my reaction to the pain.

I get a crack to the back of the head.

"Shut the fuck up!"

Tears stream from my face and drip down my neck. The arm returns and pulls me back up. Holding my breath, I limp in the direction I'm dragged. The cuts on my knees must be pretty deep, too, as I feel the warm blood drip down my shins.

Keys clang on a key ring; then I hear the opening of a metal lock. We go inside somewhere, but it's not a house or anywhere nice, as it's colder in here than outside and smells damp and dirty.

Walking further inside, I hear the voices of other men. Another Italian accent and an English man. Hold on, that's Jax's voice. A chair is placed behind me, big hands push down on my shoulders, encouraging me to sit; I do as they want. My arms are hooked and fastened around the back of the chair, my ankles pulled apart and tied to each chair leg. The hood is pulled off my head. My eyes take a second to adjust to the bright lights all focused on me.

The man in front of me is vile. If you could imagine evil personified, this would be him. Face covered in scars. Eyes dark, having seen and caused horrendous amounts of death. A wicked smile shows his gold teeth. After ensuring my ankles are tightly fastened to the chair, he runs his hands up my legs. His face comes closer and closer to mine. His breath makes me gag.

The higher his hands go, the more I panic. I switch into fight mode, thrashing about. I headbutt him, managing to get him on the nose. He's furious. He stands up, and I know what's coming. His fist hits the side of my eye with such force, I feel like my head has been knocked off my neck. High-pitched ringing in my ears, colours, and then darkness. I'm out.

Chapter 20

Leo

She lied to me. She doesn't love him. I'm pouring myself another drink when Marco appears at my office door.

"Keep a clear head. We have a busy night."

That's right. Tonight, we catch our nemesis. The ones who dared to steal from the Guerras. The delivery tonight is a setup. Lives will be lost; they will pay and be an example to everyone of what will happen if you dare to cross a Guerra.

"Don't worry about me. Find all you can on that Jaxon. I want to know everything."

"Already working on it."

"Actually. Take me to the airport; this is ridiculous."

I'm furious, but I want her back where I can see her. I want to rip out that Jaxon's eyes. I saw the way he looked at her. What was I thinking, letting her go off with him?

Marco stops me from leaving the room.

"Let her calm down. She will be back."

Will she? I'm not sure. The only thing I do know is that my head is a mess.

"Tonight, we sort the business. Tomorrow, you sort your woman." He taps me on the shoulder, leaving me to my thoughts.

She has until tomorrow to come to her senses, and then I will claim what is mine, once and for all.

Hours later, we're in the ship's cockpit, waiting for the inevitable. Everyone is ready. I have fifty men with enough ammo to wipe out the whole of Italy. This ends tonight. Marco goes over the plans one last time with the captain and crew. They are to wait in here with the doors locked until Marco or I come back with the password.

Boom. They're here. All power is cut, the engine is off, and the emergency lights take over, casting a red glow throughout the room. Marco looks even more like the devil now.

"Showtime!" Marco excitedly announces.

The plan is to wait until every intruder is on the ship. We don't want anyone getting wise to the situation and taking off. The more of them we have to torture, the more information we will find out. This may, of course, mean losing some of our men, but that can't be helped, unfortunately. Marco and I make our way through the hallway to the storage cabins where our cargo is usually kept. Only today, there's no cargo. Today, it is Marco's torture chamber. Chains hang from the walls and ceilings. Tools are carefully laid out on a table. Large equipment, like Marco's favourite, the chainsaw, are dotted around the room in full view, ready for easy access.

The first sound of gunfire echoes through the metal walls. The intermittent sound of death continues for around twenty minutes, getting louder and nearer until the first intruders arrive. Marco opens the door as he hears them approach. Two of my men bring in two men about to meet the devil. Sweating and looking terrified, the men are chained to the walls. After thirty minutes, we have ten men imprisoned. Marco can hardly contain himself; he's pacing up and down in front of the chained men, touching his tools and equipment as he passes. He's like a child in a toyshop, unable to decide what he wants to play with first.

"Good evening." I crack my neck, releasing the tension building within me. "I'm sure I do not need to introduce myself, but just in case. My name is Leonardo Guerra."

Four of the men are affected by my statement. One of the men pisses himself, another's eyes nearly fall out his head, the next bows his head as if accepting his fate, and the final one begins to cry. I know these men have been employed as extra muscle. They're not part of an organisation; they're here to make up numbers. Unfortunately for them, their number is up. The other six men scowl at me. They know who I am. They also have evil in their eyes.

"So tell me. Who sent you?" None of the men speak other than the one who is crying and now muttering something in French, I think? I will start with him. As I walk over to him, he closes his eyes like that will make me disappear. "You. French?"

The man nods, still with his eyes closed.

"You understand English well enough, though, from your reactions." I lift his chin. His lips tremble. "Open your eyes."

As he does, another cry escapes his mouth. "I'm sorry, I did not know. I have a family. I need money for food. Please let me go."

You could feel sorry for the guy. But I don't. He will have been part of the last group that invaded my ship, stole my cargo, and killed my men. Those men had families too.

"Who do you work for?"

His eyes flicker for a second to another man, confirming he is one of the original gang members.

"I do not know.... I come, get paid, go home."

He's lying, but he knows he's dead if he says anything. He's also dead if he doesn't. If he doesn't talk, I'll kill him. If he does, they will kill him. I just need to show him that not talking prolongs an agonising death. Whereas if he tells me what I need to know, I'll make it quick and almost pain-free.

I move to the guy the whimpering French man looked at.

"Are you also French?"

The man curls his lips at me and then spits in my eye. The pocket square in my jacket pocket is ready for these incidents. It's not the first time I have had bodily fluids on my face, and it won't be the last.

Once I have cleaned myself, I speak again, standing further away this time. "Who are you working for?"

He doesn't answer. But this guy isn't French. I'd guess he's English. As I expect, he stays quiet.

"Marco. Show these men I don't like ignorance. Remove his leg. Maybe that will encourage him to use his voice."

Marco smiles. He picks up his chainsaw and starts the motor. It's extremely loud; the noise vibrates in your ears. The smile on Marco's face is contagious—well, to me, it is. For the men, it causes terror. Chains rattle as the men try to get free. It's no use; they're going nowhere.

He waves the saw around him, loosening up his limbs. As he gets to the man in question, he asks. "Any last words?"

Before the guy can release his spit, Marco swings the saw into his thigh. The screeches and cries from grown men are enough to give you nightmares for the rest of your life. I watch the amputation. Surprisingly to some, I don't enjoy this part of the job.

I take in the reactions of the other men, all of whom look away. Two of them are being violently sick, and another has passed out, dangling from the chains attached to his arms. I'm disturbed from my observations by the feeling of a vibration in my jacket pocket. I pull out my phone, realising I've forgotten to switch it off. A mistake I don't usually make. Looking at the screen as I go to press the power button, the name Damien King captures my interest. The call ends, but I instruct Marco to continue while I leave the room.

Once far away from the noise, I call him back. "Mr. King. To what do I owe the pleasure?"

"Guerra. When was the last time you spoke to Katie?"

A tug in my gut puts me on high alert. "Why? Explain immediately!"

"My wife spoke to Katie as she got off the plane at Heathrow. She was supposed to call her when she got home. She hasn't."

"What time was this?"

"10:00 p.m."

The time on my watch is 3:00 a.m. So that was five hours ago.

"Check her apartment."

"I have security on that building. She hasn't returned home."

"Then where the hell is she!" My fist hits the metal wall.

Two of my men round the corner, guns at the ready, investigating the dooming echo. I wave them away.

"CCTV shows her leaving the airport. She follows Jaxon Adams down a side street where we lose visual."

"What do you know about Adams?" I ask.

"Nothing. He's completely clean. Too clean. He's just done a short spell with the police, but that's not even on his record."

"His address?"

"We've been. There's no sign of them."

Taking a minute to think, I feel panic rise in my core. I'm not in control. I'm *always* in control.

But right now, I'm in the middle of the ocean on a ship in a different country from where I need to be. Why the hell did I let her leave?

"King. I need your help." Never in my whole life have I ever asked for help.

"I will do all I can to find Katie. But I won't be doing it for you. Whatever resources you can send our way, do it now. We've eyes all over the city and are following up on vehicles leaving the area, but there's a lot to get through. The more eyes and hands I have, the quicker we will find her."

"Done. Ring me in one hour."

The call ends, and I storm back into the massacre. Marco has been enjoying himself.

"We need to hurry this along."

Chapter 21

Leo

"I think I have all we are going to get," Marco informs me.

Only three men remain alive, one of whom will stay alive—for now, anyway. This man will take the decapitated and limbless men back to where they came from. I doubt he will live for long once he arrives.

Leaving Marco to finish the job, I instruct my number two to send all the resources and men we can gather to Damien and his team. A helicopter arrives just as Marco has finished. We both board the aircraft, which takes us straight to the airport, where my private jet is waiting. A blood-covered Marco scares one of the flight attendants, but they know not to speak a word. Once he's showered, he takes a seat in front of me.

"We will find her, boss, and I will skin him alive."

Marco runs through the information we have with me and the team. We've some men on board, and the rest are present via video link. Damien is also on the call, going over things on his end. There have been no further updates. It's now 4:00 a.m. My Katherine has been missing for six hours; a lot can happen in six hours. Standing up from my seat in frustration, I pace the aisle.

"Tell me again, Marco—what do we know?"

"Jaxon Adams. Thirty-two years old. English."

There's something here I'm missing.

"The ship. What did you find out there?"

Marco looks at me quizzically but goes ahead and answers. "Four of them were hired for the job. Two French and two German. The other six are part of an organisation called Graves."

"Graves? What do we know about the Graves?"

"They're English."

There's a connection here; I'm sure of it.

"Damien. What do you know about an organisation called Graves?"

There's a moment's pause.

"The Graves were a criminal gang based in London and the US. Their boss and his son died a year or two ago. It's all been quiet since then."

"Well, they're back. Find out all you can on them."

"What has this got to do with Katie?"

"I don't know yet. That's what we need to find out!"

As soon as the plane lands, we are out, in the car, and on our way to meet Damien at the last known location of her phone.

We pull into a car park; Damien and his team are all set up with riot gear. He has a group surrounding him as he looks at a map he has laid out on the bonnet of an SUV.

"This is where Katie's phone last connected." He points to the map.

I push through the group to get a closer look.

"Everyone, this is Leonardo Guerra; he is a friend of Katie's."

I send him a glare. "Get on with it, Damien!"

"As I was saying, her location stops around half a mile from here. We have traced a transit van that leaves the airport minutes after Katie disappears to this area here. The CCTV is practically nonexistent for about a mile." He draws a circle around the area.

"We have surveillance on the surrounding areas, and as yet, the vehicle hasn't moved. As you can see, it's pretty derelict around here, bar and a few cottages dotted about. After driving around the area, we've found no sign of this van. They've hidden it somewhere. My guess is here." He points to a square on the map.

"Where is that?!" I demand.

"Half a mile up that road, there is a disused warehouse." He points over my shoulder.

I turn and can see it in the distance—a dark green metal building.

"What are you waiting for then? Let's go!" Turning on my heel, I start to make my way back to my car.

"No! Guerra. You cannot drive up to the warehouse; you will alert them of your arrival and kill us all!"

I despise being told what to do. So does Marco; he's ready to kill someone. But this time, I am going to have to listen.

"Fine. We will go on foot."

Marco and I set off walking.

"We aren't ready yet, Guerra. You both need kitting up, and we need to wait for the okay from the authorities."

I stop walking and turn to Damien. "If it was your wife, would you wait?"

He straightens in his position by the car. "Not a second more," he replies and nods.

Chapter 22

Katie

I've been in and out of consciousness, hearing bits of conversations. Jaxon is here, but he isn't tied up like I am. He seems to know these people. Although they're far from friendly in their discussions, each of them wants something from each other. Jaxon has something they want. Jaxon wants them to be part of something in return. Hours pass by, and each time I wake, I am more alert; this time, my attention is drawn to Jaxon going through my bag. He pulls out my Snuggly, my teddy.

"Jax, what are you doing?" I cry.

"Aww, look, the baby has decided to wake from her nap. Does the baby want her teddy back?" Waving it in my face, he laughs cruelly.

This is a side to Jax I have never seen.

"You and this pathetic bear. Look, it's falling to bits."

He rips his arm off. I sob.

"Why are you doing this to me?"

"Remember the morning the police raided my house? I needed a place to hide something." He rips off the other arm. "I needed a safe place where it would be looked after. What better place than this stinky old bear that never leaves your side." He rips off his head and pulls a small plastic square out of his body.

"What are you doing? This isn't you. Get us out of here, Jax. These people are bad people; you aren't bad like them. Please, Jax!" I scream as he walks away, throwing my bear on the floor and handing the plastic object to the second Italian man.

"Stop, Jax, no! Don't give him whatever that is. I've heard them talking. They're going to betray you, take what you have, but not do what you want in return."

The two Italians glare at me in annoyance.

"She speaks Italian?" the evilest one asks Jax.

He thinks for a moment. "No." He laughs.

I never did get around to telling him I was fluent. My outburst is punished with a fist in the side cracking a number of ribs. My breath is taken away as the pain of expanding my lungs rips through my body.

"Not another word, bitch!"

A fist to the cheek puts me back to sleep. At

least I don't feel pain while I'm out.

Leo

The sun is starting to come up, which means we have a good visual, but it also means we are ourselves more visible. Although Marco is an extremely large man, he is very good at the element of surprise. I, on the other hand, am not so discreet. Hiding behind a bush, I let Marco go and stake out the area. It's eerily silent, bar a few birds tweeting in the distance. I've never been a praying man, but at this moment, I pray Katherine is in here and alive. It feels like an age, waiting for Marco to return. I almost leave my hiding spot to go look for him.

"The van is inside to the left of the building. Katherine is to the right."

"Great—let's go."

"Hold on." Marco grabs my arm. "She doesn't look good. There are at least three men with her; I didn't get a good enough look at all their faces."

My blood boils, but I can take on three with no problem.

"Boss, one of them is Martelé."

"What?!" I will put a bullet in his head right now.

"Wait, we need to find out what they want. Calm, okay? Just at first. Then we rip their heads off with our bare hands!" Marco growls quietly so as not to give away our presence.

"Ready, boss?"

"Always."

Following Marco's nimble movements, I try to walk in his footsteps. We enter the warehouse without alerting anyone to our whereabouts. Once inside, we hear voices. Martelé—I'd know that voice anywhere. He just started a war.

My body has a mind of its own. Not being able to wait another second, I kick down the metal door between us and them. Not surprisingly, we are met with rifles aimed at our heads. With our weapons drawn, too, we assess the room. Blood speckles the floor, and what looks like fluff is scattered in a line leading to my Katherine. There in front of her is a torn-up, limbless teddy bear.

"Guerra! What the fuck are you doing here?" Martelé seems surprised by my arrival.

My eyes are on Katherine. My heart burns at the sight of her. Bound to a chair, her perfect body is bloodied and broken, her head slumped, too exhausted to lift at the noisy sound of our arrival.

The mention of my name by Martelé, however, has her eyes searching for mine. I see that glimmer of hope sparkle as our eyes connect.

Rage and instinct take over.

"You steal my woman, Martelé, and you expect me not to come after you?"

"Your woman?!" he splutters, looking over to his left. I follow his line of sight and see a smug-looking Jaxon Adams leaning with one foot up against the wall.

My arm automatically lifts, and I shoot him, shattering his kneecap.

He rolls around on the floor in agony. "Ahhh, you will pay for that, Guerra!"

I don't bother to reply.

The nearer I get to Katherine, the sicker I begin to feel. My heart threatens to burst out of my chest, and my ears ring.

"I'm here. You are safe now." Holding her head in my hands, I kiss her, a silent promise that I will never let anyone hurt her again. I speak softly as I untie her. "Who did this to you?"

She looks over at Martelé's number one, who stands beside him. Without a second thought, I put a bullet between his eyes. The large sack of shit drops to the floor with a thud. "Nobody hurts my woman and lives to breathe the same air!"

Katherine, now untied, buries her face in her hands.

As I pick her up, I mistakenly turn my back on Martelé for a second, missing the moment when he retrieves his number one's gun.

He now has one pointed at Katherine and one at Marco. Marco stands strong with his weapon pointed back at Martelé.

"Guerra! You do not kill Martelé men and walk away. An eye for an eye, Guerra. Who will it be?" He looks from Marco to Katherine.

Covering Katherine with as much of my body as possible, I work through solutions in my head. Martelé smirks as he waves a gun at each of the most important people in my life. Choosing isn't an option. Marco is like a brother to me. He has saved my life on many occasions. Trained and taught me how to rule and survive. He's been more of a father to me than my own; in my brother's absence, he is my best friend. I feel a bead of sweat release from my brow. I hope Marco has a plan; if anyone knows how to get out of this, it's him. We need to delay until Damien and the team arrive.

"Who will it be, Guerra? Him or her? Him or her?"

He's getting more and more angry at my silence.

"COME ON, GUERRA!"

Hurry the fuck up, Damien is all I can think.

"Him or her, Guerra. If you don't pick one, I will choose one for you! Five seconds, Guerra!"

Shit, Damien, hurry up. I can't shoot first, as he will definitely fire at Katherine; in her condition, she doesn't have much chance of survival, so I won't risk it.

"Five…. Four…. Three…. Him or her, Guerra —you need to choose. Two…."

"ME!" Marco's growl rumbles throughout the warehouse.

Guns fire. I dive to cover my Katherine. We fall to the floor, my body paralysed in protection mode. I'm frozen until I hear a whimper from Katherine beneath me. I scan the room now that the gunfire has stopped. Both Marco and Martelé lay facedown, blood pooling out beside them. Tears pour from Katherine as she sobs. Picking her up as gently as I can, I hold her head to my chest.

"Close your eyes. We are leaving now." Carrying my entire world over the top of the bloodshed, I vow never again to let her be part of this violent life. She deserves better. As we reach the fresh air and daylight, Damien and his team surround the warehouse.

"Too late, dickhead! Too fucking late!"

Katherine falls unconscious in my arms on the way to the ambulance that waits around the corner. I'm not letting anyone take her from me, so the medics treat her in my arms. I'm numb; for the first time in my life, I don't know what happens next. All I know is, Marco sacrificed himself to save me from losing the woman I love. Her safety is now my priority; I will not let his sacrifice be in vain.

When we get to the hospital, I'm forced to let her go. Katherine's parents and friend Bella are there, waiting anxiously. Painful cries leave their bodies as they witness the trauma she has suffered. Observing their pain and the love they have for their daughter, I realise what I need to do.

Chapter 23

Katie

Hospitals have a very distinctive smell. Before I even open my eyes, I know where I am. The reason I'm here floods back into my memory.

"Oh no, Marco!" I sit bolt upright in bed, and my parents put their hands on my shoulders.

"Hey, sweetheart, you're okay; you're safe in the hospital." My mother sits on one side of my bed, my father on the other.

"Where's Leo?"

"He's outside. Where he has been ever since he brought you in," my dad replies.

"Two days he's stood guarding your door; I didn't even know you two were in touch again?" my mum comments.

"I did," my dad chirps back sarcastically.

Ever since I can remember, they've had this who-is-the-better-parent competition going on. They had me as teenagers and still act like that's what they are when they're together.

"She's awake. I told you to inform me the minute she woke up!" Leo blares at my parents from the doorway. "Doctor!" he shouts down the corridor.

My mum rolls her eyes. "He's very bossy!"

"He saved your life. Do you remember what happened?" Dad asks me, concerned.

"Bits," I say, not wanting to talk about it.

Leo returns with the doctor.

"Clear the room; the doctor needs space to work," He barks.

My mum and dad leave, each giving me a kiss as they do. Leo stays, watching the doctor's every move. My blood pressure is taken, then he checks my dressings and looks into my eyes.

"Everything looks good. You're a lucky lady."

"When will I be able to take Katie home?"

"Another day or two, as I'd like to keep an eye on her for at least another twenty-four hours. If she continues to improve, she can recover at home."

Closing the door behind him, the doctor leaves Leo and me alone.

"Katie?" I question. Leo has never once called me anything but Katherine.

Pulling up a chair, he sits by my bed, taking my hand in his.

"It's the name you prefer, isn't it?"

"Well, yes." Although I'd gotten used to being Katherine just for him.

"How do you feel?"

"I'm sorry." I sob.

"No. I'm sorry. This is all my fault. I should never have let you leave. I let him take you away. I failed you."

The pain in his eyes breaks my heart. Reaching out to hold him in my arms, the pain of my broken ribs stops me; realising this, Leo climbs into bed beside me and holds me. This feels like home. This is where I want to be. With him. Safe.

"I've called off the wedding."

I feel a little sad to hear that.

"You know, I really didn't mean it when I said I loved Jax. I just said that because I wanted to go home."

"I know." He squeezes me a little harder, kissing my head.

"I'm so sorry about Marco." I thought he hated me. I can't believe he sacrificed his life for me. Tears roll down my face; he meant so much to Leo.

"Hey, don't cry. It will take more than a little bit of lead to get rid of that monster."

"He's alive?"

"Sure is. And giving those doctors and nurses hell for not letting him go home already."

"I'm so relieved, Leo." I sob.

"Me too. How are you feeling?"

"A little sore, but mainly tired."

"You get some sleep." He goes to get up.

"Please stay," I beg, holding tightly on to his hand.

"I'm never leaving you again."

That makes me smile. Drifting comfortably off to sleep, I hope he means it.

Leo is true to his word. When I wake, my head is nestled in his chest. His head rests on mine.

A lot has changed in the last few days. Having a near-death experience really makes you realise what is important in your life. Although I'd been forced into a marriage and held in a country against my will, I'd never felt so looked after, loved, and happy. Leo's lifestyle is far from ideal, but what is the ideal life? They say you shouldn't marry the person you could live with for the rest of your life. They say you should marry the person you can't live without. Leo has never been far from my thoughts since I met him all those years ago. After spending these past weeks and months with him, there's no chance my life will be worth living without him.

The door opens, and in walk my parents, waking Leo. Sitting up slightly to greet them, Leo firmly keeps his hold on me, not wanting to let me go. My dad's eyes dance between us, not used to seeing his daughter in such an embrace, and with a man he has only just met. His nostrils flare, and he clears his throat.

"Your mum and I have been talking; we think it would be best if you came to stay with me while you recover."

What a surprise; out of the two of my parents, it's my dad who has offered to take care of me.

"That's not necessary; Katie will stay with me."

My dad shoots Leo an annoyed glance.

"That is, if Katie would like?" Leo turns to face me, his eyes wide in question.

Him calling me Katie and asking me what I would like to do are all very strange statements coming from Leo, but I accept them gratefully.

"Thanks, Dad, but I think I would like to stay with Leo." It's where I feel most safe—by Leo's side.

"And where will you be staying, Leo? Don't you live in Italy?"

"In London, not too far from here I will send

you the address, and you may visit whenever you wish. It is very comfortable and will cater to all Katie's needs."

"Right, I suppose that's sorted, then." My dad doesn't look impressed.

I feel bad, but I can't be apart from Leo.

"You have a house in London?" I whisper to Leo.

"I do now." He winks.

Later that day, Damien and his business partner Josh come to speak to Leo and me.

"Have you found him?!" Leo demands.

"Not yet," Damien responds.

"Find him immediately and bring him to me! I will be the one to tear his head from his body."

"With all due respect, Guerra, you're not in Italy now. We will find him and deal with him."

Damien and Josh stand tall in front of Leo. The amount of testosterone in this room is enough to make any girl faint.

"Leo, who are you talking about?" I ask, leaning out to grab his arm, trying to diffuse the situation.

I know full well who they mean. Jax. I have

been scared to ask, not wanting to know the answer. He is either dead or had escaped. Either way, I haven't felt strong enough to think about it.

Leo growls out a huff and sits beside me, recusing himself from the conflict.

Taking my hand, he kisses it. "I will not let him or anyone hurt you ever again. I promise you. Jax will pay a thousand times over for what he has done."

"Unfortunately, Katie, when I and the team entered the building, Jaxon was nowhere to be seen. We have people working tirelessly to find him, and we will," Damien finishes, nodding to Josh to continue.

"At your request, Guerra, we have looked into the Graves. It seems you may be onto something. The Graves organisation was originally run by a man named David Graves. His empire ran throughout America and England. Although a criminal gangster, he had morals and values. His son, however, did not. Cain Graves, David's son, was the main boss throughout England, but the power went to his head. He got greedy, started using drugs, and caused turmoil within his own organisation. His father stepped in eventually, but it was too late. Many innocent people lost their lives. Both Graves men died almost two years ago. With the next heir in line not wanting any part of it, all has been quiet since.

However, it seems now that a family relative has decided to rear their ugly head. A highly intelligent computer whizz who can ruin your life with the touch of a button, apparently. A distant cousin who goes by the name of Jay, or J.A."

"Jaxon Adams?"

"More than likely. We think that the Martelés were working with the Graves."

"No, the Martelés work only for themselves, like the Guerras," Leo argues.

"Maybe so, but the Martelés and the Graves leader were both involved in kidnapping Katie. For what reason, as yet, we don't know."

"I might do," I admit.

Chapter 24

Katie

Nobody has actually asked me for my version of events yet. Maybe they don't want to upset me, or maybe they think it won't be of any value.

Starting at the beginning, I explain how the police raided Jax's house. How two men broke into his home, and I had to escape through next door's loft. I told them about the police, how that guy had been outside the salon, and how Jax had treated me since getting on the plane back to England. When I relive the details of my kidnapping, my body shakes; I can't hold in the sobs when I explain the terror I felt, the pain they inflicted. Leo's temper builds. He stands, fists clenched, before reining it in to sit back down beside me, comforting me.

"The Martelés wanted something from Jax. Whatever it was, he had hidden it in my bear." Sadness comes over me as I think of my Snuggly. "Guessing, I'd say it was a memory card of some description."

Josh is taking down notes while I speak. "Describe it to me."

"It was only small. About three or four centimetres and blue, I think."

"Good, Katie, you're doing really well. Carry on," Leo encourages, squeezing my hand.

"The Martelés wanted what Jax had hidden. In return, Jax wanted them to do something for him. I don't know what. But whatever it was, they had no intention of doing it."

"How do you know?"

"I heard them talking. They were going to take it, then kill Jax and me."

"And Jax didn't hear them say this?"

"They spoke in Italian."

Leo's attention pricks up.

Damien notices this. "Katie is fluent in Italian. Did you not know, Guerra?"

Both Damien and Josh smirk at Leo's furious reaction. Feeling bad, I look at him to explain, but he just kisses me.

"My Katie is full of surprises."

Although I can tell it is killing him inside, he lets it go. My heart swells for him in that moment.

"I tried to warn Jax, but he didn't believe me. That's when I got this." I lift my hand to the swelling on my face that surrounds my broken cheekbone.

Leo hisses in anger. "Why would they take Katie? I saw Martelé's face when I arrived. He wasn't expecting me. He had no idea I even knew Katie."

"That we don't know, but I'd guess Jaxon knew exactly who you were. He probably took Katie as insurance."

That's right, Jax knew who Leo was on the beach when they meet the first time. I was so surprised Leo knew who Jax was, it hadn't even registered.

Leo

Marco, the stubborn sod who refuses to die, is adamant he is discharging himself the day Katie is released. It's been less than a week, but he insists he is fine. Bullet number twelve. I really thought this was the one that had finally defeated him. However, I should have known. Not that I'd ever tell him, but I'm really glad he didn't die that day.

I've rented a house on the outskirts of London. Damien has sorted the best care team around to ensure they're both fit and well as quickly as possible, which is good, as I need Marco. I have an idea, and he has work to do. Marco is unhappy about my plans but goes along with them all the same. The arrangements in Italy are beginning. Part two of the plan is to get Katherine —Katie—to *actually* agree to be my wife. I'm in love with her. From the moment we first met when she was the quiet, teenage Katherine I first knew to now, the feisty Katie I grow more in love with every day. Making her happy is what I need to do. She will be my wife, but under her terms.

Both patients have their blood pressure checked by nurses. The pair sit side by side. Katie is telling Marco all about some Netflix series she is watching about the mafia. She makes me laugh, suggesting things to Marco about how we could do things. At least she is taking an interest in the family business. I laugh at Marco when he catches my line of sight. He's less than amused and furious he can't get up to leave. Katie continues twittering on regardless. Damien, Bella, and their little daughter, Daisy, arrive to see Katie. Damien leaves Bella to talk but lingers in the hallway, texting on his phone.

"Does he always follow you around like a lost puppy?" Marco asks Bella.

She laughs.

"A Rottweiler, more like." I add.

"Yes, he's never far from us. Heaven forbid Daisy and I are apart; he doesn't know where to be."

Marco tuts and leaves the room. He doesn't

understand love and relationships. In his opinion, men who put women before themselves are soft. Up until I found Katie again, I had similar thoughts.

Leaving the girls to chat, I make some calls. It seems the news of the recent deaths has made it back to Italy. Now that the Guerras have murdered the Martelé leaders, we have just declared war. It was an unavoidable situation but one I could do without. Although we have some time while the Martelés appoint their new leader, we must get back to Italy and sort out the situation. The fact that neither I nor Marco are in the country doesn't bode well.

Katie

"Any idea when you will be coming back to work, Katie? No pressure, obviously; you take as much time as you need. Just so I can make sure everything is ready for you, that's all. Plus, I really miss you."

"I've really missed you too."

And I have; I meant it. But not enough that I want to go back to work. When I look to my future now, I don't see myself here. I'm in a hot country living by the sea with Leo. There's nothing keeping here. I love my parents, but we don't live in each other's pockets. We go for months without seeing each other. And anyway, Italy isn't so far away.

I watch Bella with Daisy so happy and content.

"I think it's time for a nappy change." Bella laughs when we both get a whiff of Daisy.

"I'll change her. You stay with Katie," Damien insists, entering the room and taking Daisy from Bella.

The love in Bella's eyes when she looks at them both is moving. That's what I want. To love and to be loved. I'm moving to Italy.

When our guests leave, I hobble around the house, looking for Leo. Finding him in the dining room, his makeshift office, I wait quietly while he is on the phone.

"Van! You are part of the Guerra mafia! Not the Boy fucking Scouts! Now get out there and sort it!" He throws his phone onto the table, then looks up at me. "Hello, what are you doing there? You should be in bed, resting."

Before I can protest, Leo has picked me up and is carrying me to our bedroom.

"Will you lie with me while I go to sleep?"

"Anything for you." Leo gets in bed beside me, still fully clothed, so I know he will be slipping away once I'm asleep. There is trouble back in Italy, and I know he is eager to get back. Tomorrow I will speak to him about leaving for home.

Just as I am falling asleep, I hear Leo whisper, "Ti amo." *I love you.*

My heart is full as I drift into a much-needed sleep.

Something disturbs my rest. The time is 3:00 am. The room is dark other than a crack of light coming from under the door. Hearing voices, I go and investigate. My feet freeze to the spot when I observe the situation in the kitchen. Two men are tied to dining chairs with what look like extension cables. Their faces are bloodied and battered.

"Get here right now, Damien!" Leo walks around the room, talking on the phone. "You sort this out now before I make all this even more of your business. No police! They will either lose their heads or their legs; that depends on how quickly you get here!" Leo sees me in the doorway and ends the call.

"I'm sorry, my love. Come." He ushers me out of the room, closing the door behind him.

"What's going on?"

"Everything is okay; you are safe. These chancers just broke in, looking for something worth stealing. Marco and I caught them. It's all over.

"Leo, I know those two men. They're the

ones who broke into Jax's house that night. One of them came to the salon looking for me."

He takes me into the utility room, switches on the light, and makes a comfortable seat on the bench out of towels and bedding. "You sit here until I come back, okay? Here." He passes me a gun. "You point that at the door; anyone you don't know, you shoot. Understand?"

"Yes."

"Do you have your phone?" Leo holds his hand out.

Taking it out of my dressing gown pocket, I place it in his palm.

"He must be tracking your phone somehow. Stay put."

With shaky hands, I wait. The room must be soundproof, as I hear nothing until Leo opens the door about ten minutes later. As soon as he does, I hear a lot of people in the house. Damien and Josh are here. The men on the chairs in the kitchen have gone and are now replaced with who I can only assume are Damien's security team, as they all wear earpieces and black jackets.

"I can't protect her here. We are going back to Italy tonight." Leo looks at me for approval.

Seeing the hope in his eyes, how could I say no.

"I'm ready when you are."

Chapter 25

Katie

It's amazing how quickly you can get things done when you're Leonardo Guerra.

One hour after that very conversation, we are sat on Leo's private plane, about to take off to Italy. We would have set off ten minutes previously if Leo hadn't requested that the plane be thoroughly searched a third time, checked for anything untoward. Marco seems extremely inconvenienced by it all.

"It's for your safety, too, Marco!" Leo frustratedly fastens his seat belt.

Marco grunts, rolling his eyes.

"Why don't we play a game?" I suggest.

Marco's eyes bulge, and his nostrils flare.

"Eye spy, maybe, or cards? I think I have a pack in my bag." A necessity when traveling.

"Are you a child?" Marco huffs.

Winding Marco up is a little pleasure of

mine. Especially now that I know he doesn't actually hate me.

The flight passes quickly. For me, anyway. I've never flown on a private plane before. At the front of the plane, there are armchairs that have seat belts. That's where you sit for takeoff and landing. The chairs are nothing like what I've seen on a plane before; these are leather armchairs you'd have in your living room. The next cabin along has more armchair seats for guests. Following that is the bar area with tables, chairs, and sofas. The bedrooms are right at the back. It is a luxury I have never known existed. I even got to meet the pilot. He was quite shocked when the three of us piled into the cockpit. It was obvious nobody's ever bothered to speak to him before.

When we land, it's early morning. The sun is rising, and the sky is a beautiful violet colour. The air is already warm. I take a deep breath, and I exhale with a smile; this is where I belong. We are heavily guarded by Leo's men when we leave the plane. Cars surround ours on the way back to the house. There would have been a time when this would have freaked me out. But it no longer fazes me. I trust Leo to keep me safe. As long as I'm with him, I'm happy.

I'm greeted with hugs and kisses from Alga and Sergio as soon as I walk through the door. It's good to be back.

Leo gets me settled in the garden, my favourite spot. Alga waits on me hand and foot, feeding me all my favourite foods, never allowing me to finish a drink before the next one arrives. Spending the next couple of weeks pretty much wrapped up in cotton wool and gaining half a stone has me desperate to leave the house.

First, Leo takes me around the vineyards. I've admired them from afar every day, but this is the first time I have ever walked through them.

"We use a traditional method called pergola. This is where we train the vines to grow above in a trellising canopy."

"It's beautiful, Leo." Walking beneath the canopy of greens and browns, I admire its beauty.

"We prune, trim, and harvest the fruit all by hand. It's an old-fashioned way that takes more time, but it produces the best quality."

Next, we explore the lemons. They're unlike any lemons I've ever seen at the supermarket. "They're the size of grapefruits."

Leo nods proudly. He's so handsome. The way he talks of the process with such enthusiasm, it's clear he's really passionate about the produce.

"Unfortunately, I don't get much time to do any of this myself; I can't remember the last time I was in here."

Standing in front of him, I wrap my arms

around his neck. When I look into his eyes, he looks so tired. He works so hard.

"I love you, Leo. So incredibly much."

His eyes widen, and his face lights up in a smile, acknowledging the first time I've ever said that I love him.

"Love you, too, with all of my heart."

Our lips crash together. My legs wrap around his waist, the need to be closer to him taking over my body. He spins us around in excitement, squeezing himself into me.

Placing me down gently, he disappears for a second before returning with a blanket he places on the ground. We both lie in each other's arms, staring at the fruits above us.

"I love it here, Leo, like this—so peaceful and quiet."

"One day, my love, one day."

Sometimes Leo talks in riddles. This is one of those times. It's been weeks since I felt him inside me. Most nights, he's been out working; when he has been home, he's stayed fully clothed and held me while I slept. His gentle approach has been appreciated, but now, I'm ready to be taken care of in a different way.

With one swift movement, I straddle him and remove my dress. Staring down at him in just my bra and thong, I lick my lips.

"What are you doing?" he breathlessly asks as he looks around, checking that nobody is nearby.

"You."

Happy we don't have an audience, he puts his hand on the back of my neck and pulls me towards him. Kissing me hungrily, he flips me over so I'm on my back with him straddling me.

"Are you sure you are okay for this?"

"So ready."

He grabs my wrists and holds my hands above my head. Kissing and licking my neck, he pushes my legs apart with his own, grinding his hard length between them. Oh, how I have missed this.

"Keep your hands here. Do not move them."

I nod in acceptance as he releases his grip. He reaches under my back, unclipping my bra; my breasts release perkily, craving his touch. He sucks my nipple into his mouth, and a cry of pleasure escapes my throat. I lower my hand, searching for his hair.

"No touching. Keep them here." Grabbing both my wrists, Leo again holds them above me. "Trust me, do not move."

Leo pulls a knife out of his trousers. The blade is thick and shiny. He runs his finger gently along it, his skin splitting as easily as slicing through butter. It's not deep, but beads of blood run down his finger. He licks the blood clean, then covers my mouth with his. The kissing and taste of his blood on my tongue is so erotic. Moans and hums of pleasure escape from us as we grind to find our release.

Rising above me, he places the knife blade on my chest; the cold metal sends goosebumps across my skin. He carefully runs it down my body, watching it constantly; he licks his lips. When it reaches my thong, he slices through the straps at my hips. With one quick movement, he rips the remaining material from my body, leaving me completely bare. Feeling completely on display and extremely desperate for my man, I sit up to reach for his shirt.

"Did I say you could move?" He turns me onto my front and slaps my bum before pulling me back to face him.

The sting is delightful but just adds to my desperation for contact.

"Now, be a good a girl." He does, however, reward me by removing his shirt.

Reaching to his right he pulls a lemon from a nearby tree. After slicing it open with his knife, he squeezes it in his hands, letting the juice run down his arm and onto my body. The drips tease my breasts, stomach, and hips before they run between my legs. Leo opens me up and watches in pure lust and fascination. Feeling the vibration of his growl, my yearning ignites. My hips buck as I try not to move my arms. His head dips, and I wrap my legs around him, using the limbs I'm permitted to move to get what I need. He kisses, licks, and presses that five o'clock shadow exactly where I need it. My legs quiver as I rise to him.

"That's it, ride my face. Such a good girl."

His words of encouragement and praise have me screaming his name. Before I can recover, Leo removes his pants, and his cock stands proudly glistening, ready for action. The look on his face melts me. I'm his. Every last bit of me is his, and he knows it. With a smile on his face, he impales and claims what he rightfully owns.

"So what now?" I ask while our entwined, naked bodies recover from our lovemaking.

"You want to go again? I'm game for that." Leo climbs on top of me.

Laughing, I push myself up to face him.

"No, I mean with us. Can we still get married?"

Leo half smiles, tilting his head to one side. "When you're ready, yes."

"I'm ready now." I confirm.

His eyes narrow. "We don't have a ring."

"Yes, we do." I grab my bag, and I take out the

engagement ring he bought me when I first arrived in Italy.

"But you hate this ring?"

"I 'hated' this ring because I love this ring. This is the ring I wanted the love of my life to get down on one knee and ask me to marry him with. This is my fairy-tale ring."

Leo takes the ring from me. "I'm no good with words. But I love you. And I promise to always protect you. Katie, please, will you do me the greatest honour and become my wife?"

Surrounded by lemon trees, this incredibly handsome, powerful man is naked and down on one knee, asking me to marry him.

"Yes, I will."

Picking me up, he wraps me around him, kissing me with such love, I feel it in my bones. "Come on, let's get changed and go celebrate."

Leo takes me to the first restaurant he ever took me to with the incredible sea views. The restaurant manager is flustered as he realises Leo's table is once again occupied like our first visit.

"Mr. Guerra, I'm sorry—I didn't realise you were back; forgive me. One moment please, and I will have your table ready."

Leo stops him. "No!"

Other staff members look over in horror.

"We will sit at the bar."

Leo takes my hand and walks us over to some bar stools. He helps me get seated and then sits in front of me.

Pulling my stool closer to him, I laugh.

"What is so funny?"

"Nothing." He really has changed. Or maybe he's always been this Leo, just very hidden.

We have a lovely evening, talking and laughing, touching and holding.

"When would you like to get married, Mrs.-Guerra-to-be?"

"As soon as possible, Mr. Guerra."

Nodding, Leo taps my glass with his. "Cheers."

Chapter 26

Leo

The date is set for this weekend. A little sooner than I had anticipated, but the sooner, the better. All the plans have been pushed forward; the day will go ahead just as arranged. While Katie and my mother have final dress fittings and whatever else brides and the mothers of grooms do before a wedding, Marco and I have some business to attend to.

Damien has informed me a delivery is to arrive at one of my warehouses in thirty minutes. Hoping it is what I expect, Marco and I pack up the car with the necessary equipment and head over there. We arrive before the delivery. My phone rings as we enter the warehouse. Damien.

"Guerra, your container should be with you shortly."

"I trust it is what I expect."

"That depends on your expectations, but I doubt you will be disappointed. As you are aware, the Graves were working under new leadership.

Jay, or Jaxon Adams, is a highly intelligent computer expert. It seems he was hacking into organisations' systems and blackmailing them into working alongside him, Martelé being the most recent, with you as next on his list, given the trouble you have been experiencing lately. Thankfully we have managed to get the true heir to the Graves to come forward, resulting in the organisation turning Jay in to us. The issues, unfortunately, don't end there, but for now, we trust you will tie up this loose end in a, let's say, more deserving way than mine or Josh's morals would let us."

"I am grateful for your generosity in this, Damien. Your hard work will be repaid. I am in your debt."

"There is no debt to be paid, Guerra."

"Maybe we shall work together again in the future."

"Let's hope not." Damien ends the call just as the lorry carrying our delivery rounds the corner.

Marco and I watch as the forklift carefully lifts the container off the back.

"Don't be so careful; it's not fragile." I groan impatiently.

The driver takes the hint, releasing his fork midair and allowing the metal container to crash to the floor, then tip over onto its side with a loud boom. Once it's inside the warehouse, Marco unlocks the door to the container. It opens with a loud screech. The stench that flows out is putrid. Human excrement and god knows what else. Jaxon is crouched in a corner, his arms shielding his eyes from the sudden light. He's been in there for over forty-eight hours, apparently. After a moment he stands up and walks towards the door, inspecting who has just released him from his prison.

"Guerra!" Lunging forward when he sees it's me, he's soon put on his knees by a crowbar to the shins, courtesy of Marco.

"You will pay for this, Guerra."

"No, Jay, I won't."

His eyes widen when he realises I have called him the name he uses when working for the Graves. "Your time as a Graves is over; your time, in general, is over. How do you think we found you so easily?"

The penny starts to drop, his expression changing as he realises, he has been thrown to the wolves by his own men.

"How's Katie?" Jaxon changes the subject to annoy me.

"Don't mention her name."

"She tastes good, doesn't she? And that little moan she does when—"

Crack. My fist breaks his cheekbone.

He doesn't fight back. Instead, he laughs and continues. "She likes it hard, you know. Slap her about a bit, if you know what I mean."

Anger consumes me; my body reacts on impulse, and I beat him over and over. I must stop myself. He's not getting away with it this easily. He's taunting me. Forcing my mind elsewhere, I calm myself.

Jaxon coughs and splutters; he spits out teeth with blood as he picks himself up from the floor.

"You've seen that scar on the back of her shoulder? I put that there, biting down as I pounded her from behind." He loses his balance as he thrusts his hips for more effect.

It doesn't work, however.

The scar he speaks of I know very well. I also know he did not put that there. Katie acquired that scar one night after falling from the hotel wall when we were teenagers. We were running away from security. Katie thought I didn't want to be seen as I would get thrown out. Really it was the fact the guards would recognise me; I didn't want Katie to know who I really was. Katie and her mother would have been treated very differently the minute anyone found out they were friends with a Guerra. I enjoyed being treated as a normal person. Knowing that she was being nice to me because she liked me for who I was, not because she feared what would happen to her if she wasn't.

Surprisingly, though, she still treats me as if I were any regular guy. She's not scared of speaking her mind or putting me in my place. I love that about her. She makes me feel loved, normal and happy. I'm myself when I'm around her, a self I haven't been for many years. Unlike many of the women I have been with, Katie doesn't want to be with me because of my reputation. She wants to be with me despite it.

Jaxon continues to goad me; Marco clearly has heard too much.

"ENOUGH!" With one flick of his knife, Jaxon loses his tongue, thus ending his provocations.

We manage to keep him alive for another six hours. By the end of it, I'm exhausted, relieved it's done. Marco could have continued, I'm sure. The body and each piece of flesh we have removed are thrown back into the container to be sent to the Graves. A reminder that anyone who dares to cross the Guerras will not live to tell the tale.

Once we have cleaned ourselves up, we visit my father. He wants to know the plans for the wedding in detail. He's a shell of the man he used to be. Frail and yellow in colour, he sits in his wheelchair. Once a dangerous, powerful man who haunted my nightmares, he could now drop dead at any moment.

While Marco runs through the schedule of the wedding day, I find my mother in the kitchen. She's standing at the island, mixing some kind of cake batter. My parents have staff to cook, so I know when she's in here, it's to take her mind off something. Her eyes are visibly red and swollen. To know you are about to lose the person you love must be incredibly hard. The pain is too hard to imagine.

"Mamma."

"Leonardo. It's so good to see you." After kissing both my cheeks, she holds my face in her hands. "You look so tired. Sit; let me get you a drink."

After getting a glass out of the cupboard, she pours me some wine from the bottle she is drinking.

"How is Papà?"

"He is looking forward to your wedding."

We make small talk while she continues to beat the batter. We live in such a life of luxury. Anything we desire, we can have without limit, apart from the two things we need most—health and life. Two things which we all take for granted. Things which I now plan to cherish.

Marco appears at the door, notifying me that my father wants my attention.

I go to him.

"Leonardo, Marco has everything under control. He is a true Guerra."

"He is one of the best," I agree.

My father then holds out his arms. A gesture I have never seen from him before. He flaps his fingers, encouraging me to get closer. Assuming he must be trying to give me one last crack while he still can, I do as instructed.

To my surprise, he pulls me into him, slapping me on the back. He whispers, "You've done me proud, son." Then he releases me.

A nod is all I can give in return. Since the day my brother died, my father has only ever treated me like the monster I have become. By his hand, I have endured beatings and torture. All to prepare me for the life that I now lead.

He made me a demon.

It wasn't always like that, though. Before the death of my brother, my father and I were close. I worked with him in the vineyards, and he taught me everything I know and love about viticulture. That is the father I remember; I have already mourned his death.

"A package has arrived for you, sir," Sergio informs me as soon as I arrive home.

"Excellent; where is it?"

"On your desk, sir."

Pleased to find the package is exactly what I have been waiting for, I immediately go to find Katie. She's in our bedroom getting ready for bed.

"Oh Leo, you're home. I've missed you." She flings her arms around my neck, and I breathe her in, instantly feeling relaxed.

"Hey, what do you have there?" She tugs at the package in my hand.

"It's a surprise for you."

"You know I don't like surprises."

"I think you will like this one." I tease.

Apprehensively, she takes it from me, then slowly tears open the box. The reaction she gives once she takes out what's inside isn't what I expected. Tears flood her face, and she sobs hard.

"Hey, hey." I sit beside her on the bed. I wrap my arm around her, pulling her into me. Seeing her upset makes me crazy. "I'm sorry. Is it bad? I'll send it back now."

"No, it's perfect." More crying. "How did you do this?"

"I arranged for someone to collect all the parts and had it sent off to a teddy bear specialist. Does he look okay?"

"My Snuggly is even more special now. Thank you, Leo."

"You're welcome." I hold her for a minute while she holds the bear, counting my blessings and shutting out the thoughts of what might have been.

"Talking of surprises, you still haven't told me where we are going on our honeymoon!"

"That's the whole point of a surprise."

"Please, Leo—I need to know what clothes to pack?"

"Ahh, you won't be needing any clothes." I kiss her.

She pulls away. "Seriously, Leo, I need to know."

Using distraction techniques, I take off my shirt and pants before heading to the bathroom. As I'm turning on the taps to the bath, I feel her behind me. "You want to join me?"

Her hands come around my waist. "I know what you're doing, you know."

"Good, then you'll also know you won't win. You may as well get undressed too."

When she lifts her nightdress, I see she is delightfully naked underneath. Together we wash away my horror of a day, a day I will never think of again.

Well, maybe the bath part, I will.

Chapter 27

Katie

"It's my wedding day!"

Shouting at the top of my lungs, I wake up my mum in her bed. "Come on, get up, get up."

I'm like a child at Christmas. Next, I go to my dad's room. Leo has rented a villa overlooking the beach where we are getting married. Well, he's actually rented two. One next door as well. I insisted on not seeing him the night before the wedding; it's tradition, I told him. He wasn't fond of the idea but agreed if he could be just next door, which he is. He has rung me three times this morning already, and that's only since I woke up, not counting the numerous times in the early hours of the morning. I'm sure he thinks I'm going to change my mind.

The doorbell chimes, but before I can open it, in comes Leo's mum, Maria, followed by Alga.

"Ahh, good you're up. Alga is going to make us a nutritious breakfast. We don't want you passing out at the altar, and I am here to ensure we stick to schedule."

"Wow, Maria, you look beautiful."

"I thought the bride was the only one who wore white on a wedding day?" my mum chirps up behind her. She's a jealous cow; if only she knew what that remark could earn her. Luckily for my mum, her daughter is marrying into the family.

"Shut up, Mum; I don't mind what anyone wears."

"I hardly think anyone could upstage this bride. Plus, it isn't white; it's cream." Maria goes into the kitchen to check on Alga.

"Behave, Mum, just for one day; think about me."

She twitters to herself while I usher her into the bathroom and shut the door.

The balcony doors are open, and I can hear voices, so I go and investigate. There are people down on the beach, setting up for the wedding. Already, it looks spectacular. Chairs and white carpets are being laid out on the pale, twinkling sand. The gentle waves add the most beautiful backing sound. Excitement fills me. I look to my left and see Leo watching me from the balcony next door; he gives me a wink. Feeling like the luckiest girl alive, I run back in to hide.

"I'm going for a walk," my dad announces, gesturing to the group of women who have arrived while I've been outside.

The hair and makeup artists have taken over the living area. Maria is giving them their instructions. Once I have eaten Alga's delicious breakfast, my body is not my own as I'm brushed, stroked, pinned, and curled. It's nice being in the pampering seat for a change. I've done many brides' hair for weddings, but none for a wedding as spectacular as mine is going to be, I'm sure.

When it's time to put on my dress, my mum helps me into it. It's backless, white, and sparkles with my every movement.

"You look like a princess, sweetheart."

"Thanks, Mum."

It's even more perfect than I remember. All I need now is my husband.

"Knock, knock. It's time to go, ladies."

I turn to my dad, who stands proudly at the door, looking very handsome in his fitted suit.

"You're an angel," he whispers, holding back his tears as he walks me down to the beach.

The guests are all in their places, and the music starts to play. As we make our way to the aisle, my dad stops me.

"You know, Katie, I'm not sure Leo's only business is making wine."

"How do you mean?"

"Well, I heard some people talking earlier, and you know, he does seem to have a lot of money. I'm not sure how much the wine industry makes in this day and age, but it all seems a bit extreme."

"It's okay, Dad. I know exactly who Leo is. I trust him with my life. He makes me so happy."

"Yes, I can see that. Well, I'm not sure I trust him fully yet, but I trust you. Whatever makes you happy, sweetheart."

"Thanks, Dad."

We make our way down the aisle. There are hundreds of people here, most of whom I have never seen before. It's the way it has to be, though, and I'm fine with that as long as I have my Leo waiting for me at the end. I've only my parents here. The wedding was short notice, but other than Bella and Damien, who had holiday plans, everyone I want here is here. Even Emmaline and Alfie are sitting in the row with my mum.

Leo looks incredibly handsome in his suit, and I can tell he approves of my dress by the way his face lights up when he sees me. In that instant when our eyes meet, it's like everyone around us disappears. We say our vows to each other as heartfelt promises. Meaning every word, we are content in our own little bubble.

Once the ceremony is over, we are seated to the right of the guests to sign the register with our witnesses, Marco and Leo's mum. The instant I put

down my pen, an almighty *BOOM* knocks me off
my seat.

Chapter 28

Katie

At first, I thought it might be a firework. But fireworks don't give off this much smoke. Leo lifts me from the ground and carries me to goodness knows where; I can't see a thing from all the smoke.

"Don't say a word; just hold on to me tightly, okay?" Leo whispers.

I nod, tightening my grip around his neck. He walks for a minute or so, then sets me down. A black hole appears in the ground; the smoke gets sucked down it.

"We need to climb down this ladder; I'll go first. I'm right here, okay? You've got to trust me."

He holds out his hand, and I take it as he helps me down into the darkness. Reaching above me, he closes the hatch we've just gone through.

"Keep going; I've got you."

Leo's hands guide me down. The further down we get, the lighter it becomes. It's still dark, but I can now see my hands in front of me. Once we reach the bottom, I see we are in some kind of tunnel; there's light at one end. The floor is wet and sandy. It smells like dead fish.

"Leo, where are we? What's going on?"

BOOM Another loud noise vibrates above us. Bits fall from above our heads. Leo pulls me into him, sheltering me from the debris.

"We are in the sea's overflow tunnel."

"I can see that. But why am I here on my wedding day?"

"Two bombs have just detonated during our celebration."

"Oh my god, my parents! The guests!"

"Don't worry, everyone is fine. Well, apart from a couple of the Martelés and my father."

"What! Oh, Leo, I'm so sorry."

Noticing that Leo doesn't look surprised, I continue. "Hold on a minute. How do you know this?"

"We planned it that way."

"You planned to blow up our wedding?"

"It was the only way I could keep you safe."

"And you killed your own father?"

"It was his idea. He wanted to go when he decided. Not when some horrendous illness decided to stop torturing him."

"Okay, but I still don't understand why us being in an overflow tunnel keeps me safe. Safe from what, Leo?"

"That's the other thing. We died too."

"Noooooo. You didn't. Leo, you did not just kill us both! What about my parents?"

"Your parents are already in a helicopter on their way to the airport. They know you're safe and well, and they will be returning home to wait for your call. When the rest of the guests are told we are dead, they will be long gone."

My breathing picks up. "I think I'm having a panic attack."

"Here, sit down." Leo points to what looks like an old upside-down rubbish bin.

"I am not sitting on that in my wedding dress!"

"Just listen to me, Katie, please."

"Go on."

"Katie. Mrs. Guerra. I love you with every bone in my body. I can't hide it. It's written all over my face. My body language oozes my obsession. You are my weakness."

"And this is bad?"

"Yes. You make me weak. If I continued to lead as I did, you would never be safe. My enemies would always be seeking out the opportunity to hurt you. The leader of the Guerras must never be afraid. They must sacrifice themselves and their loved ones to protect their kingdom. Mrs. Guerra, I would sacrifice my kingdom to protect you."

"Oh, Leo."

"This way, my father dies in action. The Don dies with his wife along with the warrant which the Martelés had on him for killing their leader."

"You've got this all planned out, haven't you."

"I had a little help."

"COME ON!" Marco's voice echoes down the tunnel, his huge frame blocking the light from the opening.

"Can you run in those shoes, or would you like me to carry you?"

"I can run."

As we set off running, I overtake him, slapping his bum as I go. "I told you I don't like surprises."

"This is the last one I promise. Everything after today, you get to decide."

"I'll hold you to that."

"I have no doubt you will." He laughs.

Halfway down the tunnel, my heel gives way from the running. I don't fall, though—my husband's strong arms pick me up and carry me the rest of the way.

When we reach the end of the tunnel, Marco is standing there with Maria. Pulling her into me, I give her the biggest hug; I have no words.

Moving then to Marco, I pull him in for a hug as well. To my surprise, he hugs me back—well, sort of.

"Stay safe." Marco says when I let go. Leo then embraces Marco.

"Thank you, boss," Leo says to Marco, shaking his hand.

"Come, you need to get going." Maria ushers us on the waiting speedboat.

Leo helps me in; then he opens a hatch just big enough for us both to lie down in. We say our final goodbyes and close the door. Leo pulls me on top of him, kissing my head.

"Just me and my wife from now on."

The boat's engine starts, and we literally sail into the sunset.

Epilogue

Three years later

Katie

"Mark, look at the state of you. You're supposed to pick the grapes, not eat them," I admonish, picking up my very sticky two-year-old.

He giggles when I tickle his tummy.

"Leo, you shouldn't let him eat too many; they'll give him a tummy ache."

"Nonsense. I grew up eating them; they'll do him no harm."

Watching them enjoy each other's company really makes me happy. We have a life of freedom here. I'm so proud of what Leo has created for our little family. Rubbing my swollen tummy, I smile, excited to add another little one to our team. It's funny how things change. That day I was given the list of what is expected of the wife of Mr. Guerra, I was mortified. Never could I have imagined adhering to any of those demands, and yet, here I am, willingly following each and every one of them.

1. As the wife of Leonardo Guerra, it is not necessary for you to work. All your needs will be provided for.

I happily let Leo work in the vineyard while I look after our home and child.

2. As part of the Guerra family, you will be expected to keep to a healthy diet and exercise regime. Training will be arranged for convenient times by Mr. Guerra.

Keeping fit and healthy is something I want to do for us all. When Leo isn't working, I go for a run along the beach, and we work out together in our gym when little Mark is asleep.

3. Guerra has a reputation to uphold; you must always look your uttermost best.

I take pride in my appearance. Wanting to look good for your husband is every wife's goal, isn't it?

4. You will be expected to be available to Mr. Guerra at all times.

Oh, I am definitely available whenever my husband needs me.

5. You will attend events and must always stay at Mr. Guerra's side.

There's no place I'd rather be.

6. As his wife you will obey and respect every decision he makes.

Maybe not the obey bit, as he's not always right, but I respect him immensely.

7. The Guerra family must continue their bloodline therefore, it is expected that a minimum of four children will be born in the first six years of marriage. Two of these children must be male.

The more, the merrier. I'm at my happiest when I'm carrying my husband's child. And look at little Mark—who wouldn't want more of that cheeky face?

I can't say where we now live; I can't risk anyone finding us. But what I can say is, this island is the most relaxed place you could ever imagine. The community is friendly but keeps themselves to themselves. There are people here from all over the world. I'm sure everyone on the island is here for similar reasons to us.

Our house is beautiful, it's on the beach, it's spacious, and it has everything we need, but don't get me wrong—we live a simple life. Our days are spent on our own grounds, enjoying the outdoors, the sea, and the fresh air. We grow our own fruit and vegetables; we have chickens for eggs and goats for milk. We even make our own cheese. Once a month, we go down to the market and exchange our produce for other necessities. Life is good.

Just as we sit down for dinner, a noise I haven't heard for a long time sounds. The phone is ringing. The phone that never rings. The phone that is only for emergencies. Leo stands; he walks over to the cupboard where it's kept. I watch him intently as he answers. Reading the expression on his face, I know exactly what it means.

The Guerras.

And just like that, my bubble of tranquillity bursts.

The End for now.

Thank you for reading. I hope you enjoyed.

Next in The Found Series is Marco and Mia's story: She Found Me, available on Amazon.

Books in The Found Series:

I've Found Her
I've Found Her part two
He Found Me
She Found Me

With more to come later in the year

All books are available on Amazon

Acknowledgement

To my wonderful parents.

Thank you for your love and encouragement and for helping me believe I can achieve anything in the world.

I am so grateful you are mine.

About The Author

Joy Mullett

Joy Mullett has turned her obsession with reading into writing. Being a lover of romance with a big imagination Joy writes exciting and thrilling stories which are impossible to put down.

Follow Joy on Tiktok, Instagram and Facebook @jemullettbooks for her latest releases and updates.

Made in the USA
Thornton, CO
01/23/25 18:02:38

95d63c01-0185-43d4-a3f3-16409d32b7baR01